I0538180

Clock Strikes Two
And Other Stories
By Derek Clendening

MAUSOLEUM
PRESS

Clock Strikes Two and Other Stories
Published by Mausoleum Press

This is a work of fiction. Names, characters, incidents and places are either a product of the author's imagination or used fictitiously. Any resemblance to actual persons, living or dead, events or locales is entirely coincidental.

First Edition ISBN 978-0-9869198-0-0

For my good girl Emma Clendening: this selection of dark tales

Table of Contents

The Lonesome Child on Wysocki Street

Earl parked his van across the street and let the engine idle while exhaust fumes filled his nostrils. The sun was barely up, but he could shut his eyes and rest if nothing happened. The house was a yellow Cape Cod, the kind built around World War II, with a garage attached, a maple tree in the front yard, and an in-ground pool in the back. Nice that they can afford the perks, he thought.

But that was nothing that didn't permeate his mind each day when he sat across the street. However, he decided that he had better things to do than to envy the affluent. Most days, he tried to catch every motion, every pattern and every nuance in the house. Sometimes he dozed off, but he always snapped awake, and kicked himself for his sloth. So he kept a cup of Tim Horton's coffee beside him, and sometimes a chocolate glazed donut if he could afford it. Given his new need to save pennies, he refused to splurge.

Not that he wanted to live in the house though. His apartment felt cramped sometimes, but he had an extra room, suitable for a child, and he would upgrade even if it broke the bank. After all, he decided that someone must care enough to go gangbusters for him.

Each morning, he arrived at the house at eight, killed the engine, pulled his binoculars from their case, and watched the family's every move. He found the inside to be as refined as the outside, but he cared not for their plasma screen TV, or the DVD player in each room. He did not that a man with a black faux-hawk, dark-rimmed glasses, a suit and tie with a briefcase in hand departed at eight-fifteen each morning. Earl judged him to be in his early thirties, and aging well thanks to Tae Bo or Pilates, or whatever the hell yuppies like him did to stay in shape. That he no longer smoked a cigarette en route to his Lexus pleased Earl very much.

A blonde woman stayed behind. Were they really married? Earl wondered. Or did they just sign a contract at town hall and play house? She never left the place. Well, that wasn't entirely true, he decided. She stepped out for a variety of reasons ranging from grocery shopping to banking.

A boy with matching blonde hair also lived there. Earl decided that the color perfected him, but that the haircut to match his Dad's was lacking. Thank God. Like his Mom, he stayed home during the day. Home-schooled maybe, Earl thought, but he had never seen him open a single book. He'd never seen the blonde woman sit down with him to study fractions and integers, and had never seen a tutor arrive at the house.

Irresponsible, he thought. Bloody irresponsible. Earl couldn't fathom the idea of keeping a kid home from school and depriving him of the social skills learned from going to school like other kids. How someone fended for themselves in the workplace, or in life, after that was beyond him.

The time the mother left the house was sporadic. Some days she was out the door by ten and other days she didn't leave until after lunch. But she was always gone longest in the afternoon—sometimes up to three hours—and Earl figured it was as good a time as any to investigate.

Once, he had seen the woman lock herself out of the house, and then rummage around to find a rock near the garage entrance, where the spare key was hidden. It was one of those doohickeys that she might have bought at Wal-Mart, slipped the key inside, and allowed it to blend in with the garden.

That same day, the woman left again, and the kid chased her. She kept her back to him, ignoring him completely, which drove Earl to distraction. He tugged on his own hair and gritted his teeth to keep his anger in check. If he'd had a kid like him, he wouldn't have ignored him that way, he decided. He would nurture the child and be the best damn father in the world.

When they were gone, he slipped out of the van, checked to make sure the neighbours weren't watching, snuck up the driveway, and found the key in the rock. He slid it into the lock, turned it, and tiptoed into the house. First, he kicked his shoes off to avoid leaving prints on the carpet. Next, he wandered into the kitchen. He opened the fridge to find some Pepsi, Poland Springs water, and a head of lettuce, broccoli and carrots in the crisper. Velveeta cheese and a carton of eggs were stored in an upper shelf, and a jug of skim milk sat in the center. At least they made sure the kid ate properly, he thought.

In the living room, he almost tripped over the some plastic trucks and WWE action figures. That was the first thing he would change. Kids should have toys, he thought. They should be free to play, to be joyous and happy, but there was no reason why anyone should break their neck because he hadn't stowed his toys away properly.

But he would learn. Discipline required time and patience, and Earl considered himself to be a very diligent man.

Upstairs, he saw that the parents hadn't made their bed, had left clothes crumpled on the floor and dust on the dresser. Then he found a room that was cluttered with more toys than the living room, but the race car bed was made. Every inch of the room was spic and span, and he found a scrapbook that had 'Tanner' printed on the cover. It sat on a plastic desk, and included pictures from the day he was born up to the present day.

Downstairs, he opened some drawers, and found utility bills under the names Mike and Kerry Seaton. He wouldn't spend too much time snooping, as he knew that Kerry and Tanner could return home any time. But he made investigating the house a regular practice for weeks, until he'd gathered every crumb of information he could want to know about them.

But he couldn't do it in the mornings because Kerry left Tanner home alone. It wasn't until her afternoon excursion that he chased her to the Rav 4. Even then, she almost slammed the car door before he could hop in, and ignored his plea to be taken with her. The poor child was neglected, Earl thought. In the mornings, he had no one, nothing, save for his toys' solace.

What the hell kind of parent does that? Poor kid. Deep down, he wanted to phone Family and Children's Services on the bitch, and let them teach her how to parent properly. But he restrained himself enough to avoid ruining everything.

After a month of by-standing, Earl decided that he had seen enough. He'd prepared a second bedroom in his apartment for a situation like this, but he'd waited for the right time. He'd observed many houses, many families, but he'd never seen a pair that would neglect a child so. Most certainly not a special child like Tanner.

Earl had never acted on his plans. He simply watched, waited, investigated homes, learned family's routines, mastered their lives, but he had never had the nerve to go through with what he really wanted. He reached for a duffel bag full of clothes. They were used, but clean and had no rips in them. Maybe they weren't what the cool kids wore to school, but he decided Tanner should be grateful for clean clothes when other kids had nothing.

Ten a.m. arrived and Kerry left the house. And as usual, she left Tanner behind, alone with his toys, which made Earl want to climb out of his van and smack her one, but he refrained. Whenever anyone left the house, he pretended to scribble on a clipboard. Maybe he was a plumber, an electrician or general contractor employed by the high school, they might think. Chances were excellent that they hadn't noticed the van at all. Earl decided that people like the Seatons were too wrapped up in themselves to notice the little things.

When Kerry's Rav 4 pulled out, and signalled a right turn at the stop sign, Earl paused. Then he slipped out of the van, prowled up the driveway, and found the key hidden in the rock. Everything was working according to routine. To him, it was now or never, and he meant to make good on his chance.

I'm coming, Tanner, he thought. *Don't you worry. I'm going to show you a life you could only have dreamed of.*

*   *   *

Earl glanced over his shoulder as he slid the key into the lock. No one seemed to be watching. In all the times he'd snuck into the house, he'd never done so with anyone home. He wondered if he should've donned a mask, or devised an intricate escape plan. Just when you think you've got it all figured out, he thought and almost laughed. But he found nothing else about this to be funny.

He tiptoed up the breezeway tile to a door that led to the kitchen. The door was also locked. Why Kerry would bother to lock the inside door was a mystery to him. Unless Kerry figured that Tanner was safe in the house so long as both doors were locked. Flawed logic at best, Earl decided.

From the living room, he heard the sound of one plastic toy smacking another plastic toy, and the sound of mouthed missile strikes before each smack. Maybe Tanner had pitted two of his toy trucks against one another, and was now deciding which one should win. With any luck, he might put his toys away when he was finished rather than leave a mess. Then he paused, sucked in a deep breath, and tried to steady his hands before he proceeded.

One foot pivoted on the linoleum, he inched up to the living room, and showed his face. The point of no return, he thought. Then he approached Tanner, shadowed the child, and watched his jaw drop when the kid stared up at him. First he froze and Earl paused. Upon his first move, the kid screamed. He curled up, rolled backwards, hopped to his feet and dashed for the stairs. Earl chased after him, caught his ankle, and dragged him down a few steps.

Earl didn't want to be rough, but he couldn't let him run away, struggle, create a commotion, or anything else that could foil his plans either. But Tanner screamed, kicked, squirmed and tried to scramble away, which left Earl with little choice but to use force. With a free hand, Earl pressed a finger to his own lips and shushed him. And Tanner calmed. By God, it actually worked!

"It's okay," Earl said. "I won't hurt you. I'm a friend. A stranger maybe, but definitely a friend. I'm here to help you."

"You're not gonna . . . you know . . . ."

"Not gonna what?"

"You know, the sick stuff strangers do on TV? I saw it on *Oprah*! You're not gonna do *that* to me, are you?"

Earl froze and dared to think that it was the most insulting comment he'd ever heard. Why does everyone presume a man who rescues a child his own way is a pedophile? he wondered. No matter, he would show Tanner otherwise.

"You have my promise I'll never do anything to hurt you, especially nothing sick." Earl raised his right hand. "See that? It means I really mean it. Guaranteed."

Tanner struggled again, tried to scramble upstairs and drove a heel into Earl's belly. All the air evacuated his lungs. Earl caught his wind and clamped his hands on Tanner's legs. "You know what tough love is?"

Tanner shook his head.

"It means I might have to do some things that aren't very nice, but it's for your own good. Just like if your parents spank you when you're bad. They don't love you any less, but they've got to do it, get what I mean? Try and keep it from happening 'cause I don't want to do anything remotely unkind."

Tanner quieted and Earl felt relieved. As much as he endorsed discipline, it really would have hurt him more than it would Tanner to bind his wrists with nylon rope, and lead him to the van like a common prisoner.

Earl slapped him on the shoulder. "Buck up, kid! We're going to a wonderful, magical place!"

Tanner rolled his eyes.

"Fine, so it's not such a magical place, but it's a heck of a lot better than what you've been living in," Earl said. "Trust me."

And Tanner followed Earl without a word. No more kicking, no more struggling, and no more insults about sick things that he might try and do. Apparently he hadn't been taught not to talk to strangers either. Earl locked the door and returned the key to the rock, so Kerry would think Tanner had vanished into thin air.

Earl fired up the engine. Where they would go he hadn't decided. He'd planned so much in intricate detail, but he had only dreamed of moving to step two and actually succeeding.

"So Mister, where'd you come from?" Tanner asked.

"No need to worry about that. You just think about all the bright days ahead."

"You got a name?"

Earl almost told him to call him Dad, but he supposed he'd experienced enough change for one day.

"Just call me Earl for now," he said.

"Okay Earl, where do you think you're taking me?"

"You've got an awful lot of questions for a little guy," he said. "You should learn to trust me and let the rest take care of itself."

Tanner nearly rolled his eyes again, as if to say that he'd done and heard everything, and that Earl could stick his patronizing tone where the sun doesn't shine. Earl would never understand why come kids thought that they knew it all.

And he didn't want to be evasive, but Tanner had simply asked too many questions, and he was in no mood to field them all right now. As far as he was concerned, he was Tanner's elder, he knew best, and that the kid should be satisfied with that.

He'd filled the tank for a long drive, so he wouldn't need to worry about stopping for gas. Eventually, they might wind up at his apartment, he supposed, but for now they would drive as far out of town as he could manage.

By one p.m., they stopped at a diner along the highway. It was small, but full, and Earl smelled cooked meat the moment he cracked the window open. He took it to be one of those mom and pop places that had a menu to die for. Nothing wrong with that.

"Bet you're hungry." Earl rubbed his hands together.

Tanner didn't answer.

"Got a problem?" Earl asked.

"Ain't you got your own kid?"

Earl slammed the van into park. Ain't ain't no word, he wanted to tell him, but refrained lest Tanner roll his eyes at him again.

Why Tanner would say something so hurtful when he was just trying to give him a better life stunned him. But he decided that his behaviour could be fixed. Earl's hands trembled as he reached for the duffel bag stuffed with clothes.

*   *   *

A waitress in a red apron and ball cap arrived with two cheeseburgers and fries and two chocolate milkshakes while Tanner was still in the bathroom. These bathrooms were located around the corner of the building rather than inside the restaurant itself, which must be a burden in the winter. He sucked on a fry and watched the window to make sure Tanner didn't try anything funny.

And Earl had taken every possibility into account. Tanner could tell some random stranger that he'd been kidnapped and beg for help. And, even if he found no one, Earl was hard-pressed to find a kid of any age these days that didn't have a cell phone. He could be in that bathroom phoning his parents, or worse, the cops.

Now that he thought of it, he wished he had made Tanner turn his pockets out before he sent him to the bathroom to change. Sweat wept from his brow and his armpits while he constructed his own doom. He hated that he could face consequences in spite of his good deed. When Tanner returned, duffel bag in hand, Earl expelled a deep breath, and his heart settled. Tanner dragged a chair up, and Earl expected him to fawn over his fattening lunch, but he only picked at his fries. No salt, no vinegar, nothing.

The shirt clung to Tanner's body enough to show a strip of skin above his waistline. The jeans clung to his legs so much that even Earl felt uncomfortable. They'd been perfect when he'd bought them twenty-five years ago, he thought. Maybe Tanner wouldn't find them stylish—he never saw kids with Mickey Mouse t-shirts anymore—but he wasn't about to rush out and buy a whole new wardrobe. Still, he had a closet-full of older clothes that he might grow into.

Earl finished his lunch and waited for Tanner who had taken only one bite out of his burger. Earl had ordered it without onions, lettuce or tomatoes since that stuff grossed kids out. To hell with it, he decided. He grabbed Tanner's milkshake and they retreated to the van.

Minutes later, they passed through Toronto. Orillia was another hour away, but they would be free from familiar faces. He couldn't commit to it as a final destination though. Not until he knew they would be safe.

"So, where do you think you're taking me?" Tanner asked.

Earl wondered why he could think of nothing better to ask. "Your new home," he answered. And when he decided where that would be, he would keep Tanner posted.

"What was wrong with my old one?" Tanner asked.

"They didn't love you. Your Mom and Dad, I mean. Not nearly enough, not the way you or any kid deserves. Not the way I can."

"But they've always been there when I've needed them. Like when I fell off my bike and scraped my knee. My Mom still leaves my nightlight on every night."

"But your Mom . . . she just leaves you every day."

"My Mom's never left me."

"Oh yes she has," Earl said. "Don't tell me she hasn't. I've seen her do it."

"My Mom has *never* left me!"

Earl raised a hand to Tanner and he quieted. Not that Earl could ever bring himself to hit kid the kid, but he needed to block any more wise-guy comments.

"I guess you're gonna be my Dad now?" Tanner asked.

"Guess you could say that, sure."

"Am I gonna have a new Mom?"

Earl's head drooped. "No, your own Mom will always be your Mom, I suppose."

"How 'bout brothers and sisters? Am I gonna have any of those?"

Earl wanted to pull over, slam the van into park and . . . he didn't know what he would do. Scream maybe, but he didn't know what kind of example that would set. Instead, he said, "You have a brother. His name's Joey."

Tanner perked up. For a moment, he saw a flicker of hope.

Then he tuned Tanner out. Why did he have to bring that up?

He remembered how stunned he had been by the prospect of divorce. While his and Barb's split had been peaceful, he had been no less disappointed and no less hurt. And he knew that they shouldn't have pulled the plug after they had been so deeply wounded. To him, they should have been one another's support system.

Earl had hoped that the days spent together in the hospital would bring them closer together, then he worried that he had been naive. In the final days, they had taken shifts, so they hardly saw one another at all, except when one was coming or going. The house was a constant mess because no one was home to clean up, and Earl always tripped over things in the middle of the night.

Then Earl remembered how he had stuffed tissue in his pockets to fight the nosebleeds at work. He would sneak in catnaps during breaks and lunch and coffee had become more of a staple than he wanted it to be. When he splashed water onto his face and stared into the mirror, he swore that he looked ten years older.

And then one morning Father Morrigan arrived with a Bible tucked under his arm. Earl knew why he had shown up that morning of all mornings. After everything he and Barb had been through in the last few months, how could he not?

After Morrigan knelt over the bed, closed his eyes, and said a prayer, the nurse inched in, unhooked the machines, and pulled a sheet over the bed. Barb clung to his arm, and he held her for what felt like hours while they cried. He didn't want to leave the room, but he knew that they must.

When he and Barb had split, he wondered if their pain could have been avoided had they only made the right moves. What if they had done something differently? he always wondered. Or could they have done anything more?

Most of all, Earl remembered the love that he'd had to give, and his promise to offer it to a child who needed it. And he meant to hold fast to his convictions, especially now that he could give Tanner a better life, but doing so with his conscience clear seemed impossible.

"So, I'm going to have a brother, right?" Tanner asked.

Tanner's eyes opened wide. Earl turned away, unable to look at him without considering all he'd done in the last six hours, or the last six months for that matter. He found the first gap in the highway he could use to make a U-turn and dart back to the Niagara Region.

* * *

Earl mulled over how he would return Tanner through the whole drive down the Queen Elizabeth Highway towards Fort Erie. Part of him wanted to drop him off at the house if he would promise not to tell anyone about him, what kind of van he drove, what he had done, and where they had gone. But Earl refused to be naive. He knew that actions like his were never easy to unravel.

Sweat trickled down his temples and he wiped it away with a damp tissue. He decided not to duck from his actions. If anything, he meant to face Tanner's parents, to make eye contact with the people who he had spied on for months, whose home he had violated, and whose son he had kidnapped. As awkward as the situation would be, he knew that he must do it, if only for himself.

"So, where do you think you're taking me?" Tanner asked.

Earl thought the kid sounded like a broken record, but he decided that he had also underestimated his intelligence. So he evaded the question, since he didn't want to bargain with him over how this would end. He wanted to pull the plug his own way, to be a man, and face the music.

"Guess you don't want to tell me, huh?" Tanner asked. "Figures. You just want to leave me in the dark."

"No one's ever going to leave you in the dark, buddy," Earl said. "I just need you to understand a few things: First, no one is going to hurt you. How can anyone want to hurt an awesome little guy like you?"

Tanner turned to him, smiled then turned back to stare out the window.

"Just so you know I'd never hurt you either," Earl said. "Understand? Hurting kids is one of the worst crimes in the world, if you ask me. I could never do that, not to my own kid, not to anyone else's either."

Tanner nodded and Earl's heart slowed.

Earl hopped off the highway at the Gilmore road exit and drove towards the river. He had come to know the side streets and ventured through them en route to the high school. Finally, he pulled up in front of Tanner's house, and drew a deep breath. Several hours of rehearsal over the drive back hadn't prepared him for this moment. He knew he couldn't excuse his actions, but he hoped that the Seatons would indulge him enough to hear his explanation.

Once he killed the engine, he patted Tanner on the knee and said, "Stay here a minute. Got something to take care of, I'll come get you when I'm ready."

The idea that the child would sit still when he was this close to home seemed ludicrous, but it wouldn't ultimately matter. He left his seatbelt buckled and stared out the window. Earl almost visited the side door the way he and the Seatons were both accustomed to, but he turned and inched towards the front door instead. He knocked, stuffed his hand in his pockets, and waited.

The door swung open and he stood face to face with Kerry Seaton for the first time. He awaited the sound of her voice. At first, her face lacked an expression and then she sighed and relaxed. Maybe she was relieved that she hadn't opened the door to a Jehovah's Witness, he thought. But she ought to look more worried, panic-stricken.

"Hi." She smiled. "Um hello, what brings you here, sir?"

"Ma'am, you don't know me . . . but I know you and your family all too well."

She perked up, but didn't panic. Just a harmless kook off the street, she must have thought.

"Mrs. Seaton, you're not going to like anything I'm going to say, but I have a confession to make. I've been spying on you and your family for months, right from the driver's seat of my van out there. Go ahead and call the cops right now, I insist, but I still need to get all this off my chest."

"You've been spying on us?" Her voice remained steady. "And how do you know my name? How does any of this . . . ?"

"Like I said, sitting in my van every morning . . . I did . . . I just . . . . You should call the cops and have me put away. I did what I did with a purpose. I took your son away from you."

Kerry's lips parted, but her jaw didn't drop. "I don't know what you're talking about. You must have the wrong family."

Earl shook his head. "Nope. Wish I could say I that I do. All I *can* say is that I'm guilty of kidnapping and I'm more ashamed of that than anything I've done in my entire life. It's just that I needed . . . all I wanted was a second chance to—"

Tears flowed from Kerry's eyes, and Mike Seaton approached and threw his arm around his wife.

He said, "I don't know who you are, but you've got a lot of nerve standing in my doorway and upsetting my wife like this. You couldn't have kidnapped our Tanner anyway."

"Our Tanner's been taken away from us, all right," Kerry said, "but three years ago, and not from some sick bastard like you."

When Earl glanced back at the van, Tanner had vanished. The kid hadn't kept his promise, he thought. Earl gripped the porch rail, stepped backwards while Kerry Seaton cried, and cringed when the door slammed shut. He couldn't imagine the pain that the Seatons had experienced . . . except he realized that he *could*. And just then, he decided he couldn't live without answers.

In the days and months that followed, Earl watched the house from the high school, sans the van, sitting in the grass, with his binoculars at the ready. And he saw Tanner in the living room each morning, playing with his toy trucks, while Mike and Kerry Seaton passed in and out of the room.

Family Ties

The only sensible question I can think to ask is *why did you stroll back into my life?* I mean, it's not like I sent an invitation, and not like our relationship has been anything better than frigid. Yet here you are. When I saw you, I wasn't sure how to react. Frankly, I was too troubled to spit out any words. I knew 'Daddy' would've turned you off and even 'Dad' sounded too warm. I figured 'Father' was the best I could say, and you'll just have to live with that.

In addition to the whirlwind of emotions, countless memories rushed my psyche like a tidal wave. Memories are such funny things, aren't they? Time stood still when I saw you. Though I remember everything about you, I think your smell stands out the most. That distinct tobacco reek that filled my nostrils every time you lit a cigarette was unmistakable. Du Maurier. I can't even see that brand at the 7-11 without thinking of you.

Next, I think of the plaid shirts that you favored, and the stubble that you sometimes wore because you skipped shaving on weekends. Then I remember your large, tombstone-like teeth that were impossibly yellow. I used to wonder when one of those suckers would fall out, but you managed to show up the dentist time and again. That is, until I was a teenager, and apparently longer.

When I saw you, my mind raced back to being nine years old. You taught me to play the piano. 'Taught' seems like too strong a word. What you did was sit me at the piano bench and rap my fingers with a ruler each time I made a mistake. Every child should be a prodigy and master *The Marriage of Figaro* before their tenth birthday, after all. Welts on my knuckles, blood on my fingers and tears in my eyes meant nothing to you, Father.

But that was nothing, I suppose. In fact, it seems like a mercy compared to what you did to Josh when he came home with Fs on his report card. Dyslexia is a tool of the child psychologists, you always said. I still remember how you would take him out back, and how I'd had to cover my ears to tune out his screaming and crying. And I remember how he'd always had to stay home from school the next day.

And you never conjured up contrived excuses for his teachers, I'll give you that. Yours were never the falling down the stairs or walking into the door diatribes that got parents charged. No, you made sure Josh stayed home at least a day or two then sent him to school as healthy as a horse. No questions asked. And you're lucky Mom (rest her soul) didn't work, so you never had to make excuses to her bosses for missing work.

Of course, I never missed a turn as soon as I was old enough (or, old enough in your eyes). Saying that nothing I did was ever good enough for you would be an understatement. In fact, I'm at a loss to articulate that feeling. The day I told you I didn't want to play the piano triggered my worst beating. The first time I brought a report card home short of straight A's was more merciful, but still . . . . Fortunately, you spared my face and left no visible marks.

I shudder to imagine how you would've reacted had I dared to bring a boy home. Looking back, I wish I could've rubbed it in your face. Alas, I was never afforded that chance. If I had been, you might've spared him the charm that you've poured on for so many, and exposed your true self.

And then came the day you walked out on us. I never understood why exactly. But it was funny, given that it hadn't been for another woman. You never had other women, which came as a shock to Mom, Josh and I. You weren't the typical alcoholic bad father either, which I also remember thinking. But I remember the fifteen year old girl I was when you slammed our front door and on your life with us.

What triggered that, I wonder? You made it clear that you were the king of the castle and that you'd be the last one to go. Were we not perfect enough for you? Mom waited on you, hand and foot. Josh was as good a son as he knew how to be, and as good a student as he could manage (dyslexia and all), and I finally mastered *The Marriage of Figaro*. I shouldn't have believed that your jacketed back as you walked away was the last that I would ever see of you.

And you might be in for a surprise now, Father. But I didn't want you to leave. I didn't want to see you walk out the door.

Sure, those close to us (in other words, those who knew the real you) insisted that it was for the best, that we were finally free. I shed no tears, but if I had, I know that each of them would have told me that better days were ahead.

But that wasn't how I saw it, not in the beginning, at least. To me, your walking out on us was the cruellest thing that you ever did. Yes, there were the practical matters that you left behind, like how Mom had to take care of Josh and me with zero help from you. And you sent no card to say where you were (no kidding). Mom never could fend for herself and the bank foreclosed on the house.

But that was okay by you, I suppose. Men like you always find a way to justify their neglect. You didn't live there anymore, Mom was no longer your wife, and Josh and I might as well have been bastards.

No, what made your swan song so awful for me was that you gave up on us. Even in your knuckle-rapping and ass-beating, you were still willing to accept our flaws and move on. When you left us, I knew that you weren't willing to weather us anymore. You had thrown in the towel.

I'll have you know that I survived the rest of my teenage years without you, and even earned a B.A. from Brock University, and went on to earn my Masters in English Literature from McMaster. But I suppose you saw the diplomas on my wall.

I have a teaching gig at the community college that I love, but you seem to know all about it. You even learned my phone extension at the office, though you should've known that I wouldn't want to hear from you. I guess one can access any information they want these days. Oh joy!

My home is mine because I count my pennies and because I'm responsible. I don't plan to lose it the way you lost our house for us.

But it's lonely here. Divorce sure wasn't a pleasant experience, but you couldn't know about that, since I've tossed out every picture of Peter I had, wedding photos and all. Disappointed much? I guess everything I know about keeping a marriage together I learned from you.

The divorce happened first, swift and peaceful. After Mom passed, I decided that I was completely independent for the first time in my life. But boy was I in for a surprise. Like I said, here you are.

As I reflect, I ask again: *Why did you stroll back into my life?*

*   *   *

When Lorraine, the English department's administrative assistant, told me that I had a call from my father on line one, I dismissed it as a joke (albeit a very cruel one). But line one on my phone had been flashing, so I figured that there must have been some substance to it.

So I decided to pick up the phone to make sure. All I heard was heavy breathing. I don't know why that should've convinced me it was really you, but it was enough to make me slam the receiver down.

I refused to cancel my afternoon classes that day. Going home early because of you would have been like admitting defeat, and I'm well beyond that. So I kept on, struggled through my classes, and hoped that my students wouldn't notice my whirlwind of emotions.

I worried you would be waiting for me in the hall after I finished class. And don't say that it's ridiculous, because you'd already phoned my office, panting like some kind of pervert. And I've had friends whose parents have suddenly shown up at their workplace (much to their horror). Alas, the hall was devoid of you.

When I returned home, I saw the lights on inside my house. The smell of Du Maurier cigarettes struck me before I was the even halfway through the door. That you knew where I worked (and phoned my office for Chrissakes!) was bad enough. But that you knew where I lived, and knew how to sneak into my house, panicked me enough to phone the police. And that you would sit in my house and smoke your filthy cigarettes was an insult.

I mean, how fucking rude is that? Hey, did you hear that one, Dad? I just said *fuck*.

In spite of my anxiety, I didn't phone the police, not immediately anyway. Why? Frankly, I didn't know what to tell them, and I wasn't prepared for their reaction. No signs of a forced entry, the spare key back in its hiding place, and no missing property. All I had to prove that you were here was the rank smell of tobacco (and no cigarette butts were left behind, very smart, Dad).

When I dressed for bed that night, I knew I wouldn't sleep a wink. Not when I knew that you were out there, that you knew where I lived, where I slept. You seemed intent on picking up where you left off, to exercise the same iron-fisted control over my life that you had twenty years ago. Somehow, my eyelids grew heavy, and I drifted into a light sleep.

And then, the click from the doorknob turning startled me from sleep. I opened my eyes and there you stood. At first, I thought you were something from a nightmare. *A bit of underdone potato, a blot of cheese,* Ebenezer Scrooge would've called you. But your smell of Du Maurier cigarettes wafted into the room, powerful enough to wrinkle my nose. You wore your plaid shirt and showed your yellow, tombstone-like teeth, and whisked me back to the girl I used to be.

At first, neither of us spoke, but I wasn't interested in anything you had to say. Chances for reconciliation died years ago. I told you to get out, but you wouldn't leave. Then I told you to get the *fuck* out (there I go with that word again), but you were intent on staying. Before I could try and throw you out, you leapt onto my bed, wrapped your fingers around my neck, and squeezed. My windpipe shrunk, I gasped for what air I could steal, but the room went blurry.

Why you walked back into my life after all these years was a mystery to me, but I suppose you had a reason. If it was only to lay one more whipping on me, I suppose . . . I suppose I shouldn't have been surprised. But you shouldn't have been stunned that I would fight you. After all, I'm a grown woman and too proud to take your whippings. So you released your grip and paint-brushed my face, if only to keep me at bay.

Was I going to sit there and take it? Hell no! Once I broke free from you, I crawled to my cell phone and called the police. To their credit, they showed up on my front door within minutes. They noted the bruises that had blossomed on my arms and neck, and the red marks and scratches on my face. An officer stayed with me while the other probed the house for you.

But could he find you? Oh no, you managed to evade the officer that night, just as you bested police trouble when I was a girl. I gave the officers your description. The first one scribbled it on his pad, and promised to try his best to find you, but I think he was humoring me. Sometimes the bad guy wins.

The beatings continued most nights, and I gave up on police help. Some nights, you broke up the monotony and expanded your interests. One night, you sat beside me at the piano bench, and I wore welts on my fingers once more. Blood dried between my fingers again. It wasn't that I couldn't play *The Marriage of Figaro* for you (how could I forget?), but because I play the popular music that disgusts you. But I don't cry anymore. If I can cling to one thing, it's my strength.

Sometimes I like to be flippant. I've asked you why you walked out on us, but you never answer. Silence was often your way of solving problems. Silence and violence. Lovely combination, wouldn't you say?

Other times, I've asked you if you've ever visited Mom's grave. I don't press the issue, because I know you won't answer, and because I feel lucky to have escaped the usual whipping with my life. I won't take risks when I'm right on the cusp of finding out.

I don't want you in my life, but what can I do? I've considered moving, but I know you'll find me wherever I go. You'll just welcome yourself in, make yourself at home, torture me, and find ingenious ways to cheat the cops.

And yet I know that moving might be inevitable. The college has placed me on probation thanks to all the days I've called in sick. But what am I supposed to do? I can't well show up for class looking the way I do after you've really gone off. You don't spare my face like you used to. At least you wait until I'm home to torture me and no longer phone my office. What few words you say anymore you use to tell me that I'm much saucier than I was when I was young.

But it's time to take the gloves off. Oh, you might be bigger and stronger than me, but you can't break my spirit. You've hit me for the last time, you've hurt me enough, and I'm determined to banish you from me life. It's time I became completely independent, and free of you.

*   *   *

Every time I think about leaving, I throw some books and knickknacks into boxes, stuff some clothes into a suitcase, and arrange to cancel the utilities. But I stop myself, because I know that you'll follow me out this door, to a new house, to a new town, but I can't go on like this.

I'm not sure what you want from me. Maybe it's the perfection that I'd been unable to achieve as a child, or I could simply be your whipping girl. Me, I think you're after the tears that I never shed, and the remorse that I never felt. Don't hold your breath.

I clipped the obituary when I heard the news. I was twenty-two, young, but that meant nothing to me. The part of me that wanted a clear conscience pushed myself to attend the burial, but I couldn't bring myself to face it. Josh wouldn't go either, presumably for the same reasons, so I won't beat myself up too much. Still, I can't help but think that attending would have prevented my current situation. I'm not one to live with regrets, but that one I would do differently if I could turn back time.

That's supposed to be therapeutic for many, but I doubt it would have been for me. Speaking the words, recounting our history, and demanding you leave is the only way to end this, to banish you from my life. Words are the only way to exorcise the demon. So, I'll say it once more, for the final time: Get back into the ground. Leave me alone, Dad. Stay the fuck out of my life.

Clock Strikes Two

Trish lay back on the couch and closed her eyes the way Dr. Tilbe had insisted, but she always squirmed and tossed, unable to settle. Like the bed she'd slept in these last six months, this was unlike her couch at home. She could doze off on that thing. The bed in her room was a far cry from her queen-sized bed with extra pillows and the fare couldn't compare to the food that she could whip up on her own stove.

Dr. Tilbe sat at her desk, with her back to Trish, and she wondered what the good doctor was scribbling this time. Such moments made her cringe, like the worst was coming, except she doubted that things could be any worse. Whenever her blood pressure was taken, her numbers always reached the fringe of hypertension, but were never too high, and she couldn't calm herself enough to achieve a favorable reading.

Then Tilbe swung around to face her and showed the shock of red hair that reminded Trish of Medusa. Why in God's name anyone would wear their hair that way on purpose was a mystery to her and why she herself had obsessed over it seemed like a better question. The woman never smiled either. She'd had elementary school teachers with her demeanor who'd endeared themselves to her no more than Tilbe had. If only the woman could crack a smile, show some teeth, or some sense of humanity now and then, Trish might've warmed up to her.

In her hands were a stack of photos. Not the pictures, Trish thought. She didn't want to see those goddamned things again, but Tilbe would force them on her. Trish gritted her teeth and readied herself to behold them. Sometimes one must do unpleasant things in order to make progress in any relationship, she decided.

"Remember these?" Dr. Tilbe flashed the pictures before her.

"Could never forget them."

"That right? Just a few months ago, you refused to admit that these things had even happened."

But that's not entirely true, Trish thought. She wanted to snap at the doctor, but then she remembered that restraint was part of compromise. She wanted to politely remind Tilbe that she hadn't denied that the events had happened, but rather she had denied responsibility for them.

And to her, that seemed perfectly reasonable. Each time she'd seen the pictures, she'd gasped at the blood, the guts, brains, severed limbs and faces with their jaws and eyelids dropped open as if she'd seen them for the very first time. And she did feel genuine regret about the incidents, in spite of who was responsible. Life was a gift. But if Tilbe had said that she had been an accomplice to the photo's images, and that others had sworn to it, then an argument was useless.

A good interrogator could make someone accept blame for the Holocaust, Trish thought. And, as far as she was concerned, Tilbe would have found a better home on the police force than she had as a head-shrinker in the booby hatch.

But if her crime had been what others had said it was then why wasn't she in prison? Not that she minded that necessarily. She had been condemned to a place that was more undignified than any slammer. She could have committed the acts that others had insisted she was responsible for, she decided. She had been presented an option, a question, and she had acted on them. Of course, she had given a riff on that story to Tilbe, lest she be forced to spend any more time there.

Tilbe's lips parted. "When you see these pictures . . . how do you feel?"

"Every time you show them to me, it's like I'm seeing them for the first time. I don't know what to think, don't know what to say. And then I remember that they were real people with families and I know I couldn't ever face them. Not even if I didn't have any control over what happened."

"But when we first started meeting, you spoke about making decisions. Decisions that seemed very simple but turned out to have complex and awful consequences. Think you would've made the same decisions again if you knew what would happen to these people?"

Trish nodded, but she couldn't form the words against the surge of tears. She'd learned what people like Tilbe wanted to hear. They were all tricks of the trade.

But part of it was true. If she could switch places with the victim's loved ones, she would understand their hatred for her. Having accepted some responsibility for their fate had landed her in a cushier situation, she knew. But whether or not she would rethink those simple decisions was something separate. It might've sounded selfish, but she wouldn't pass up the opportunity that they had given her for anything.

When Tilbe stowed the photos away, Trish hoped to God that they would stay in her desk drawer. The doctor tapped her pen on her knee and stared down at her.

"I'm a bit relucatant," Tilbe said, "the way I always am unless someone has shown absolute contrition or rehabilitation. But I think you've shown enough of both to move on to the next step."

Whatever the hell that really meant was lost to Trish, but she assumed that it was a good thing.

"We're not done here," the doctor continued, "not by a mile. But I think we've reached a point where we can start treating you on an out-patient basis and let you start piecing your life back together."

Hip-hip-fucking hooray! Trish thought, but she wouldn't be flippant, not even if she'd only thought it. Things were starting to look her way and she refused to be her own worst enemy.

"So I'm letting you go home on a trial basis," Tilbe finished. "There are some strings attached. For example, we will monitor you closely until we feel comfortable with letting you go. And Troy will be part of the rehabilitation process just as he's always been."

Troy had stood by her throughout the entire ordeal when other men might've wished her a fond adieu. Troy, who had asked her to marry him, had set her on a pedestal, and worshipped the ground that she had walked on, had inspired her to recover and become whole again. Her situation had changed their relationship, but hopefully not their love. The idea that they could resume their life together, despite the strings attached, felt like a dream but she worried that she couldn't do it.

When she considered what she had experienced, and the wonders that she had known, she doubted that resuming their lives together could be done so easily. She worried that they would be a shell of their former selves, and that pretending like nothing had happened would be futile. Still, if it got her the hell out of this place and back into her own bed, there was nothing she wouldn't do.

"Right now your personal belongings are being packed and Troy will be by to take you home." Tilbe rested the pen on her desk. "I know you're anxious to get back into the world and be productive again, but you'll need to stay home and stick with the medication schedule you've been on."

Trish wouldn't dare defy Tilbe if it meant that she could sleep in her own bed, wear her own clothes and eat her own mashed potatoes. She nodded to assure the doctor that she understood.

"Thank you." Trish could barely force the words out or the tears back.

"I know how hard this is going to be for you," Tilbe said, "but you've made ample progress, and you're ready to rebuild your life. I believe in you."

That Tilbe could see her off with a warm remark sounded ridiculous, but she accepted it.

If Tilbe was right about one thing, it was that her life would be a bitch to rebuild, but she knew that she must try. She would scrape and claw in spite of the man in the top hat who had come to take her soul.

*   *   *

Troy pulled the Lexus up to the hospital's back door no later than one o' clock and had worn a suit and tie though he later told her that he'd cancelled his classes that day. The very sight of him holding the passenger side door open for her made her hope that life could return to normal.

His brown hair still hung down to his bangs, which no doubt still triggered his mother to ask him when he'd break down and get a proper haircut lest he be mistaken for own of his own students. His almond eyes stood out now that he wore contacts and they reminded her of the man that she'd fallen in love with. Moreover, she noticed the man that'd stood by her through every trial, every nightmare and heartache, in spite of the threat to his reputation. That she couldn't return the favor gnawed at her, made her feel unworthy.

But she banished that thought the moment he stepped forward to greet her. His arms wrapped around her, held her tight, and she felt the curve of his pecks beneath his dress shirt. She rested her head in the center and thought that she might doze off standing up. He held her hand when she stepped into the car and motioned for her to sit still while he shut the door. Still, the rainy ride home was driven in silence save for the wiper blade squeaks.

At home, every room was black, but she felt at ease when Troy switched some lights on. While she'd wished for friends and family to jump out of the darkness to surprise her, she was glad for the alone time with Troy. Hospital visitations had given their relationship a twist and she was relieved that they needn't pretend to be a couple any longer.

Fluffy, her favorite orange fur ball, curled around her leg, purred and let her know that she hadn't been forgotten. Trish tickled Fluffy's head and thought that she'd missed her more than anyone.

Trish sat at the dining room table, her hand supporting her head, with her elbow planted on the table. She drummed her thigh with the other hand. Troy had fixed spaghetti with chicken parmesean, garlic bread and red wine—her favorite—and she wanted to be thankful, except that cooking had been her job before she'd gone away. But she stopped before he would notice. She wouldn't do anything to hurt him.

"Up for tenure in two months." Troy broke the silence and wrapped noodles around his fork. "Hope the meetings'll go well enough and that my stick-up-its-ass department will be happy with my publications."

Trish smiled but was lost for a reply.

"If I can get it," he continued, "we won't have to worry about anything anymore. Mortgage, car payments, student loans, you name it, it'll be wired. If you need to stay home, you can do it, and it won't hurt us a bit."

Trish smiled and pecked at her wine. "I know, honey. Here's hoping those full professors can part with those sticks."

Tenure or not, she remembered how much Troy had wanted her to stay home in the first place. Troy was no chauvinist, or even old-fashioned, but he'd always regarded her like a china doll, and seemed unable to risk chipping her paint. Dollars and cents were convenient, in her estimation.

Maybe he was worried that some man at work would sweep her off her feet, whisk her away to paradise, and that he'd never hear from her again. Surely Troy wasn't that insecure, but she figured that everyone must have their hang-ups.

Now she worried that Troy would have more reason to keep her indoors, and everyone else out, if only to protect her.

With the dishes stacked in the sink, they retreated upstairs, and Trish found her bed looking as clean and fluffy as it'd been when she'd left. Troy chased her beneath the covers, kissed her cheek and her head then hugged her arm. Comfortable sleep wasn't all that she'd missed in her time away.

Troy started with her buttons, like he'd always had, removed her shirt and unhooked her bra. He slipped out of his shirt to show the pecks that'd cradled her head before, which were almost devoid of hair. His hands seemed to encompass her entire body when he rubbed her, starting with cupping her hands.

Next, it was her turn. She slid his blue-with-white trim briefs down to his knees and let his dick spring back to smack his stomach. Then she climbed on top, let her legs hug his hips, and slid down onto his length. While Troy grabbed her hips and bucked, she held her breath and clamped onto her nipples. Troy's quick release told her that he'd saved his energy, and he used his fingers to help get her off while they lay beside one another.

After a shower—one with shower gel and not those terse soap bars they had at the hospital—they slipped into their pajamas, hopped back into bed, and switched the lights off. Trish didn't try to sleep and neither did Troy. She'd always cherished nights like these, which were spent side by side in bed, close but rarely speaking.

"Welcome home, baby," Troy whispered.

Trish patted his wrist.

"I know we've got to take things slow, but I really hope you'll want to wear this again."

He opened the nightstand drawer, pulled out her engagement ring, and slipped it onto her finger. She let her ring hand go limp, but she hoped that Troy wouldn't notice.

She'd had to turn in all her jewelry when she'd entered the hospital, including her engagement ring, which irked Troy more than it'd bothered her. In fact, she saw an upside that she'd kept quiet about. That he'd kept it by their bedside all this time told her that he hadn't forgotten her promise, and that she had one more hurdle to pass.

Troy closed his hand over hers, kissed her again, and she cringed at the touch of his lips. Why in God's name did he have to be so mushy?

"I know this will take time and I have all the patience in the world. I just want you to wear this for now and promise me we'll walk down the aisle sooner than later."

Her eyes squeezed shut, she doubted that she could make that promise, but she knew that she must. A solid promise to Troy would raise the barrier between their lives and the other side, she knew. With this pact, she prayed that she could resist the most powerful temptation of her life.

In its own way, this was another decision with consequences, but she decided that she must right the wrongs that'd happened. Troy deserved to be happy too, she thought, and wearing his ring would meet him half-way.

If this was her life, she decided to accept it. She already lived with her share of torment, but she supposed that she deserved it. Everyone must make decisions, ill-advised or not, but she remembered how precious little say she'd had in so many important decisions.

Had she known what her worst decision—albeit her most pleasurable move—would cost her, she wouldn't have opened the door that day. Despite the endless knocking, she would have hid beneath the covers and pretended like no one was there.

*   *   *

All Trish could think of was how much she'd wound up like her mother. Not that Mom had been the picture of ambition, but she'd been a slave to her husband, and had never been allowed to spread her wings. Maybe slave was too strong a title to assign to what Troy had made her, she decided, but it seemed close.

She wasn't sure what her own ambitions were, but she'd never planned to sit alone in a house all day, with some cleaning, dishes, cooking and maybe a load of laundry to break the monotony. Troy had never been the macho, dominating man that one would associate with the attitude that a woman should stay at home and let her man bring home the bacon. But he had a swagger about him that could convince her to play along with whatever he asked. She knew she wouldn't be at home right now if not for that.

Whenever she felt nervous, she twisted the engagement ring on her finger, despite the obstacle that the diamond created. But Troy despised the habit, so she avoided doing it in his presence. She saw no reason to feel nervous right now, but Troy was on campus today, so she twisted away. A wedding date had been set, and she longed to be his wife, but she worried that boredom would consume her. Being at home was just a compromise, she told herself, and decided to live with it.

But it wasn't all bad. She wouldn't admit to Troy—or to herself for that matter—how addictive daytime television had become, or how much she loved her favorite shows (or her stories, as her Nana used to call them). A day job would rob her of that joy.

When the clock struck two, and *One Life to Live* hit the air, the migraine that'd flirted with her all morning finally attacked. Better to cut it off at the pass, she thought. She popped some ibuprofen with a glass of cold water, kicked back in the recliner and closed her eyes.

As she drifted off, she heard a knock at the door.

She hadn't been expecting anyone, but people liked to drop by unannounced. And that was okay given that she felt no need to welcome them in with open arms. If she ignored the caller, they would just go away, and she could fall back asleep.

But that would be easier said than done given that the knocking picked up, fast, rapid and hard. At first, she thought that the Jehovah's Witnesses had become persistent little buggers, but she couldn't picture them being so assertive.

Her hand on her forehead, she staggered to the door and planned to give the caller sweet shit for interrupting her nap the moment she yanked it open.

But she wouldn't do that. *Couldn't* do that seemed more appropriate because, opposite her, stood a man of about thirty who reminded her of Gary Oldman in *Dracula*. But he didn't cut her sentence off at the start; she simply couldn't speak a word.

First, a defence mechanism.

Trish said, "Sir, if you're selling something, I really don't have the time or the energy right now. I'm tired and I've got a terrible—"

"Let me assure you, ma'am, I have nothing to sell." His voice sounded so smooth, so silky. "But I do have everything in the world to offer."

With that, he stepped right past her, strolled into her living room, and seated himself on the couch. And he spread his arms out on the cushions like angel's wings. What kind of rude fucker does something like that? she thought. Had he been anyone else, she would've called the cops or thrown him out on his ear personally.

But why the hell should she have made an exception for this guy? She didn't know him. Sure, he seemed different, intriguing even, but she didn't even know his name.

And then he kicked his feet up on her coffee table like he owned the place, stretched and burped. Was he doing this just to annoy her? Even if he meant to be a pest, she found something about his grin, about his entire package, very appealing.

And that alone drove her crazy. Troy had kept her eyes from wandering for years, but much had changed for her when he'd slid that ring onto her finger. She even considered taking it off in front of this guy, but she felt too guilty to take the risk. For now, she had to make sure no one had seen her let this guy into her house. God forbid that Troy be given a reason to feel insecure, she thought. He would literally chain the front door.

When he glanced up at her with those *What's for lunch, Mom?* eyes, she thought he was adorable, and wouldn't dream of throwing him out. Still, she must know who he was.

"You've got a name, don't you?" Trish asked.

"Thomas Remington at your service." He stood up, removed his hat, and took a bow.

Trish smiled. "I'm Trish. But I'm sorry Thomas: don't you think walking right into someone's house and plopping your ass down on their couch is pretty weird?"

"Why that's only because you didn't ask me to do it sooner, my dear. I know you wanted me to come, even if you didn't know it yourself. I know a lonely heart when I see one, and you looked like the loneliest of them all. I just had to come and cure that little problem for you."

So you were stalking me? She wanted to ask, but called the words back before she could add *you weird little fuck* to the sentence. But somehow his intrusion didn't seem like such a violation. If anything, she thought it made her day more interesting.

"Oh, I wouldn't say I'm lonely." Trish closed the blinds. "Just a little bored. Nothing exciting ever happens around this place."

"Then say no more. I can show you a world of excitement you've only ever dreamed of."

A used car salesman's line, she thought. Still, she couldn't deny that his straight-forward attitude had caught her attention, and had made her even more curious about him.

He stood up and took her hand. "You're a smart girl. Such a very smart girl. As such, I'd like to put a scenario before you. Say you didn't have to live this way. Say your life could be as interesting as you want to make it. What would you do?"

"I don't know." She sighed. "I love my life the way it is, my life with Troy . . . except for that one thing, I guess."

"You mean being in this house?"

"Yeah. Yeah, that's it."

"And suppose Troy doesn't ever need to know about your little decision?"

Trish tried not to let her nod look definitive. "I guess that could work out okay."

When Thomas leaned in to kiss her, she pressed her body up against his. His tongue snaked deep into her mouth, and he caressed her more passionately than Troy ever had. She felt his sandpapery cheeks pressed against hers and reached around to squeeze his ass. Then he lowered her to the floor and made her feel weightless.

Thomas slipped her out of her jeans and panties without fumbling over a single button or zipper. She felt compelled to pull her shirt off and unhook her bra, which painted a wide smile on Thomas' face. Now it was his turn to get dirty. When he dropped his pants, his dick stood up straight and pointed at her. Trish felt rotten, not just because she was cheating on Troy, but because she was enjoying Thomas' love more than she enjoyed his. But not even guilt was apt to quell her pleasure.

Trish swore that an electric current had bolted through her body the moment Thomas burrowed into her. As he bucked, and his skin slapped hers, he hit every tender spot, but this seemed like more than what even a skilled lover would do. Thomas knew her inside out, knew her soul. When he finished, Trish lay beside him on the living room floor, and let him kiss her. She didn't know what'd happened, but she was positive that her free will had been lost.

But that was okay. She liked it that way.

*   *   *

Fifteen more minutes? What to do? Waiting for Thomas to arrive reminded Trish of first date agony, in which either person might agonize over whether the other person would show up, if they would like them, if there would be a second date. Thank God those days were behind her. She'd checked her watch every few minutes in anticipation of two o' clock, the time that Thomas had promised to see her again.

But she knew that she could count on Thomas. He wouldn't let her down.

As for Troy, she'd slept all last night without a care, though she would've expected to have beaten herself up for it, for practical reasons if for no other. She'd hidden yesterday's romp from him fairly well, if she did say so. That she hadn't let on for a moment that anyone had been in the house, or that she'd had the best sex of her life without him, seemed like a moral victory. She'd even wanted to drop him a hint about the affair, just to tease the poor bastard, but she wouldn't act too cocky.

Of course, Troy had wanted to make love before bed like usual—he'd used the tickle-under-the-arm routine to signal it—and she'd obliged if only to keep him from becoming suspicious. The sex had been stale—compared to Thomas' expert fucking, that was—but she knew how to weather that too. If she could shout, moan, and writhe enough, she could convince Troy that he was giving her the best lay of their relationship.

She checked her watch. 1:59. Any goddamn minute now.

She'd left her blinds open because she didn't want to make the neighbours suspicious. But then she decided that suspicion was part of the fun, part of the risk, part of her reason for doing this. Of course, she couldn't leave Thomas himself out of the equation. A daily dirty visitor sounded like fun, assuming that he wanted to be that visitor. Such a friend would break up the monotony of her daily life and add a dose of excitement.

At exactly two o' clock, Thomas stepped through the front door, removed his hat, and took a bow. That he hadn't knocked this time didn't surprise her. If he would stroll into her house without being invited, there was no reason to knock when he was being invited, she supposed.

Thomas took her hand, kissed it, and then kissed her lips. "Twenty-four hours without you has been far too long, my sweet."

Why the hell couldn't Troy say stuff like that? she wondered. She tried to brush it off and enjoy Thomas' words.

"God, I thought two o' clock was never gonna come," Trish said.

"Then it makes our time together all the more worthwhile." That grin appeared on his face again and Trish nearly melted.

Thomas seated her on the couch, brushed his leg against hers, folded her hand in his lap, and kissed her once more.

Though it pained her, she meant to stop as she wanted to learn who Thomas really was. The mood that he created surely wouldn't be marred by stopping to fire a few questions at him. Like where he lived and what he did for a living. Fun was fun, and she saw no reason to engage him in a deep conversation, but she decided she should know something of his background.

"Thomas, I have to know something," Trish started. "Who are you? I mean, where did you come from? Why come to me?"

Thomas paused and grimaced, like it pained him to talk about it. She withdrew in case his story was something awful or traumatic.

"I'm a man without a story, without a life." His head drooped.

Trish perked up. "What does that mean?"

"I still don't know who my real parents are, never have seen a picture of them. You see, I was adopted . . . a few times over, I'm afraid. I had a family once but then that family didn't want me anymore. Too much of a burden, I suppose. And then the next family couldn't keep me because my father couldn't stop beating my mother."

Trish's hands cupped over her mouth. "My God Thomas, that's awful."

"And that's how my whole childhood went. Different day, different family. Showed up to school with a different last name every year. I was passed around like a basketball, never treated like a real child."

She took his hand in hers. "My God, that's awful. Kids should never be treated so horribly."

He nodded and stayed mute. A tear rolled down his cheek and she wished she'd never broached the topic.

"I'm sorry, Thomas," Trish said. "I didn't mean to open an old wound. I just wanted to get to know you better. You forgive me, don't you?"

"Of course I do. I could never be mad at a beautiful girl like you." He stroked her chin. "Besides, I'm not here to worry about me. I'm here to worry about you and only you. I know you're having a devil of a time in this life of yours, but it's nothing that can't be fixed. What can I do to make it better for you?"

"I'm not sure if there's anything left to do. Nothing you haven't already done for me, that is."

Thomas smiled, patted her hand.

"I mean it," Trish said. "You've already made my life more interesting considering my everyday has gotten so boring. You've given me something to look forward to in the afternoon besides the soaps. Like I finally have a purpose."

"Ah, then let me give you more purpose, and make your life even more fun. How about I come and see you every day?"

She nodded and pulled him in close.

When he leaned in to kiss her, she felt compelled to shed her clothes again, like he could sexually command her. She wouldn't fight him. He started by shedding his own clothes and then helping Trish with hers, until they were on the living room floor again. But that was only foreplay. For sex, they adjourned to Trish and Troy's bed. Trish felt rotten about that one, but she couldn't let poor Thomas make love to her on the living room floor. Not after everything he'd been through. He deserved more.

Deep down, she wanted to let Thomas move in with her. She could stash him away in the basement or attic and could visit him any time she wanted to. He would be a dirty secret to keep from Troy, but she knew it would never work.

"For now," Thomas said, "we must keep our friendship a secret from everyone. Enjoy my company as much as you'd like, but you'll want to keep it quiet for your own good."

She hadn't expected Thomas to put it that way. A real lover, she would've imagined, would snatch her away from her husband, and whisk her away to some far off, magical place. Thomas had done the latter, but she wondered why he would talk sense to her like that. Didn't he want to live with her in paradise?

"But we *are* going to run off and live together, right?" Trish asked.

"Trust me, sweetheart, we're already joined together. We're one flesh. Nothing else matters, not even your Troy. But there are still some small matters to see to, some decisions to make."

"What decisions?"

"You'll know soon enough, my dear."

* * *

A close call had come and gone. When Trish and Troy had hit the bedroom, she noticed that Thomas had left his socks behind. Two black balls scrunched up on the door. Troy might assume that they were his, but she kicked them under the bed anyway. Risky business was one thing, but she wouldn't spit in the wind.

But if they were Thomas', had he left the house with shoes and no socks? He could have slipped on a pair of Troy's worn socks and been none the wiser. And, if he did, then Troy would be missing a pair of his own. But she wouldn't worry. She would find a way around that. So far, she was proud of the secret she'd kept.

Sex with Troy had been just as bland as she'd expected. No foreplay, no entertainment, nothing to spice it up. He seemed only to want to climb on top of her and pound away without the least consideration for her needs. Not like Thomas. He saw to her every whim and always made lovemaking an event.

Book in hand, Trish curled up on the couch and tried to read, but the lines were blurry. And she glanced up at the clock too often. 1:45

led to 1:46 so slowly. Any more than fourteen more minutes to wait until Thomas arrived for his daily visit and she would go crazy.

Then finally, the door opened, and Thomas appeared with a package tucked under his arm. The package was gift wrapped in Christmas paper. He looked mischievous, like he'd derived some guilty pleasure in buying her something, wrapping it up, and finally giving it to her. Like the Grinch in reverse.

He set it on the chair then reached out to hold her.

She leaned in, kissed him, and it erased all her thoughts about last night's forgettable sex with Troy. In a real man's arms, she saw far less need for a husband, and more need for a lover.

Thomas smiled. "It's been far too long, my sweet."

"It's been less than twenty four hours."

Trish tightened her grip around Thomas' neck. "Why do you say such sweet things to me?"

"Just because you're you."

For once, Trish wanted to be the aggressor, and show Troy some expert lovemaking. How she would do it mattered less than her will to succeed. She took his hand, meaning to lead him upstairs, but he didn't budge. She yanked this time, but he refused to come along.

Thomas' expression was stoic and she wondered what was wrong. Had she said something? Made the wrong move?

"Something wrong, Thomas?"Trish asked. "Why won't you come to the bedroom with me?"

"Oh, I want to see your bedroom again. And I want to be inside you again. All day long. But there are things we must take care of first."

Trish tried not to pout like a child, but struggled to keep her chin up. She wanted him to follow her upstairs so she could lay him as he'd laid her. When he didn't comply, she wanted to stomp her feet. But she didn't want Thomas to think that sex was all she wanted from him. She wanted him to know that she enjoyed his company, his wit and charm, and his place in her life as much as what they did beneath the covers.

That meant she must give in to him, at least for now. She decided she would work up the energy to fuck him to smithereens some other time.

"Okay." She drew a deep breath. "What matters have we got to take care of?"

"Well, there is one thing." He reached for the package. "A project I've been working on for some time."

"You know, this reminds me," Trish said. "You never did tell me what you do for a living. So, what are you? An international man of mystery?"

Thomas smiled. "I do all sorts of things and most of them have to do with helping to shape lives. Helping people become stronger by learning to make decisions is where I excel. Call me a counsellor if you will."

Thomas set the package on the coffee table and pointed at it the way Vannah White pointed at the letters on *Wheel of Fortune*.

"Now, you go ahead and open that," he said.

Whatever it was, Thomas had whipped up something special. And sometimes little surprises were equal to sex, she thought. Not better. Never better. But they were always pleasant.

She tore the paper off and found a plain General Mills box beneath. Then she peeled the packing tape back, opened the flaps, and found a device with a red button inside. No Styrofoam, no newspaper. Just a device on its own without cables or wires.

And so she lifted the device, held it before her eyes, and wondered what the hell Thomas' big idea was. Surely this was some joke, or he had something ingenious in mind? She only smiled and awaited Thomas' explanation. The explanation didn't come.

"I'm flattered, Thomas . . . I think . . . ." She smiled so she wouldn't hurt his feelings.

He sat her on the couch and wrapped his arm around her. "Doesn't look like much, does it? It's okay, you can say it. Looks like something you'd play Nintendo with. Nothing to interest a grown woman. Anyway, you might not know it, but handy little gadget it your ticket to freedom."

She thought that Thomas himself had been her ticket to freedom, but she didn't mind some added insurance if she could have it.

Thomas took the device. "You see, this isn't some ordinary device. It's a machine that will help you to execute your will, on anyone or anything. You must be willing to make a decision. Sometimes decisions are hard to make. You know that. Other times they're impossible. But you must make them and be willing to execute them. This device will give you some serious leverage."

"You'll still be here even if I decide I don't want to push the button, right?"

"I'll be here as long as you want me here. That's the part of your decision-making power, my sweet. You say the word and I'm out the door. But I know you really don't want it that way. You want to use your power for good, for us."

Trish nodded.

Again, she considered the device's missing wires. How could the button transmit information? Was it connected to anything by satellite means? And what exactly would the button do? She'd seen movies in which a button opened a trap door or delivered an electric shock to some unsuspecting boob. And that was fun and laughs. This was serious. She couldn't press the button without knowing its consequences.

"So, if I press this button . . . what happens?" Trish asked.

"Think of the button as a metaphor, my dear. You only need to press it, to take the first step. Much like the first step you need to take in life."

"What about Troy? Will he still come home if I press this button?"

"Only if you want him to. Nothing you don't want to have happen can be if you're making your own decisions. You hold all the cards."

Total control, complete autonomy, was what she'd longed for since she'd met Troy. And now she could have both. So long as no one got hurt, she saw no reason to withdraw.

So she regarded the device again, drew a deep breath, and pressed the button.

*   *   *

When Thomas arrived the next day, he carried a suitcase and looked to be in a hurry, but he assured Trish that he wasn't leaving her. In fact, he proceeded upstairs to dig her suitcase out of the closet and stuffed it with clothes. And he didn't forget little things like her toothbrush, her special conditioner, and her makeup. Would he finally whisk her away to a new life? She wouldn't be that presumptuous, but a girl could dream.

Trish stood in the bedroom door. "Thomas, I know you like being direct and all, but . . . what the heck are you doing?"

"I asked you if you'd like to take a trip together sometime." He didn't look up from the suitcase. "You said yes, you named the place, and I promised to make it happen. Just making good on my word, my dear."

Again, Trish was unsure how to respond. Yesterday he'd asked her where she'd love to go for a getaway. She'd answered with a weekend in Toronto. Nothing far away and nothing extravagant, and yet she'd given it no thought. It'd simply been the first idea to enter her mind. Besides, she thought he'd brought it up to her as something they might do in the future. Maybe they'd never do it at all. She hadn't expected him to follow through on it in under twenty four hours.

That she hadn't been given a chance to pack, much less get her hair done or buy a new outfit, drove her nuts. Still, Thomas' thought was what mattered and she wanted to appreciate his effort.

"Thomas . . . I don't know if I can just go away with you on the fly like this. I mean, if I just leave for a couple of days, no explanation, no nothing, Troy's gonna know all about us."

"Why you said that's part of the fun. Didn't you?"

"It *is* fun. You know, because we can dangle the affair over his head, and let him be suspicious, but never able to know for sure. If he can prove it, I don't know what'll happen to me. Maybe he won't marry me. He might kick me out of the house."

"But you shouldn't worry about any of those things. You pressed the button yesterday so you ought to feel powerful. At the very least you should be at ease about those little worries."

Trish resigned herself. She had considered how much pressing one little button would change her life, and yet she doubted the change could be so dramatic. If she left, Troy would immediately notice, and Lord knew how he would react. He would probably call the police and all of her friends and relatives. At the bare minimum, he would be worried sick, and unable to forget that she'd taken off on him.

On the other hand, part of her didn't give a damn about Troy. If he hadn't cooped her up in the house, she wouldn't have needed to break free. She decided that she could be whisked away this weekend—whether Thomas knew it or not—and she was determined to make it worthwhile.

And so she packed the remainder of her necessities and hopped into his car. Thomas didn't even harp at her over what she considered necessary for the trip the way Troy did. Thomas drove her to a boutique inn near downtown Toronto, which was attached to a pub that was packed with University of Toronto students. But in spite of the inn's comfort, he wouldn't let her out anywhere. Having lived so close to the city her entire life, she'd seen all she'd ever wanted to see in T.O., but she still wanted to escape for some fresh air.

But it wasn't all bad. The entire inn was designed Victorian style, so the rooms were unique, unlike what one would find in a five star hotel. Their room included a queen-sized bed (and what looked like a hand-sewn quilt), an antique writing desk, and a claw-foot bathtub. Trish was glad to stay in a room with such character if she was allowed to roam nowhere else.

To Trish, Thomas' behaviour was off-kilter. She'd noticed how his fingers curled tight around the steering wheel on the drive up. He'd stared straight ahead, eyes on the road, the whole time and had hardly uttered a word to her. For a guy who'd been so slick and smooth before, his unease caught her off guard.

When they arrived, he lugged their bags upstairs himself, then opened his laptop at the desk and typed for better than an hour. The screen didn't flash Yahoo! Mail or anything likeminded. What he was working on was a mystery to her.

Just when she thought Thomas had become as possessive as Troy, he freed her for dinner at a bar and grill across from Union Station. The menu was appetizing and Thomas relaxed when dinner arrived. He ordered a second glass of wine, stretched and grinned. Yet Trish could help but wonder what was up.

Back in the room, they showered together, but resisted temptation. Trish waited on the bed in her black lace teddy—Troy's favorite— while Thomas brushed his teeth. She told him she would gladly take him with a gallon of wine on his breath, but he insisted on attention to detail.

Thomas switched the room light off, but left the nightstand light on. Trish loved the glow that shined on his torso. Then he slipped beneath the covers, kissed her lips, and ran his finger up her naked arm.

"I know it's hard to see the city lights from this room," he said. "Wish I could show them to you. But you've got your freedom now. You can see anything you want for yourself. You've begun to grow already and the fact that you're on this trip proves it."

Proves it how? She meant to ask. Maybe because she didn't care what hell she might've put Troy through by doing it? But she wouldn't upset Thomas. She wanted to trust him. Having pressed the button on that little device meant that she could grow as a person, or so she wanted to believe. Maybe it wasn't anything the button did. Thomas had taught her that life is a metaphor, and that she needed to take an important step.

Given that, she felt like she could take another important step. She remembered how badly she'd wanted to give Thomas the best fuck of his life and how the chance had passed her by. Lying in bed, he still looked slightly uneasy. Now seemed like the perfect time to capitalize on her leverage.

"Thomas." She whispered in his ear.

"Listening, my love."

"You've had something on your mind this whole time. Don't tell me you haven't. What're you thinking about?"

"Your new life and how much you've changed already." His smile looked forced. "Amazing the difference one decision can make, isn't it?"

Trish pressed her finger to Thomas' lips and he spoke no more. Then she kissed him and pulled his shirt over his head so hard that it nearly ripped. A new environment would spice up the sex for both of them, she thought. Not to mention the idea that the guests in the next room could hear their pants and moans.

She slid onto his hips, down onto his cock, and rode him. Normally Thomas did all the work from start to finish, and always left her satisfied. Now he was silent save for a few grunts and moans. His arms pinned to the mattress, she wondered if he'd pulled the whole button thing to turn the tables and get the best fuck of his life. But she doubted it. Enhanced sex was simply a bi-product of her new freedom.

When they finished, she lay back and stared up at the ceiling, blankets and sheets askew, with Thomas drained. Trish decided that she'd done a great job, but she hoped that he would have enough energy for a second round. Most of all, she loved having a lover and would do anything to keep him.

And that was but one decision that pressing the button had helped her make.

*   *   *

Thomas' BMW vanished the moment he dropped Trish off. Better that no one could see who'd brought her home, she decided. As she strolled towards the front door, she felt rejuvenated, like the weekend had added years to her life. Thanks to Thomas, she didn't have a care in the world.

Inside, she found Troy pacing what might become a giant hole in the linoleum kitchen floor. His hair was frazzled and his face was rough with stubble. A pair of bloodshot eyes coupled the creases beneath.

Trish set her bags down. "So, how was your weekend?"

"My weekend? My *week*end?" Troy threw his hands up. "How the fuck do you think my weekend went?"

"I'm just asking because I care, dear."

"I'll bet. You just packed your bags and took off to God knows where without telling me a goddamn word! I've been sick to my stomach, I've hardly slept a wink, and I've been waiting for the police to call with some sort of update."

"Troy, you actually called the po*lice?"*

Troy's face reddened, and his cheeks puffed out like a chipmunks, like he could hardly restrain his words. "You're shitting me? What the hell else does a guy do when he comes home and finds his fiancé missing? No note, no phone call, no kiss my ass, nothing." He glanced at her duffel bag. "Bet you've been having the time of your life while I've been worrying myself sick."

"I've been gone but now I'm home in one piece and you've got nothing to worry about." She strolled past him to grab a Poland Springs from the fridge. "Don't be so dramatic."

When he turned back, she found him in the hands-on-his-hips pose he used to show her he meant business. She expected him to blow up, to scream at and maybe strike her. But he abandoned the stern act, took a deep breath, and pretended not to care. Like he didn't give a shit what she did. She thought his passiveness was nearly as bad as hers and she didn't appreciate the one-upmanship.

In bed, he said nothing to her, but that was fine. A perfectly good couch was made up downstairs and Trish didn't give a damn which one of them slept in it. She broke the silence by flipping the television on, but Troy's face stayed buried in the pillows. Truth be known, she wanted to piss him off a little. She'd been trying to get his goat since the kitchen fight, but he wouldn't budge. What more would it take?

And so she watched the news. She turned the volume up just to try and wake Troy, but gave up after the first chorus of snores. On the TV, a slender, dark-haired woman in a trench coat stood before a red brick bungalow that Trish knew, with police tape tied around a maple tree. Red and blue police cruiser lights flashed in the background.

Her name was Rhonda Simmons, she held a microphone like a baton, and she announced that an entire family had been slaughtered and the police were without a suspect. Trish had seen such scenes on CNN and thought they were vultures for covering human misery 'round the clock. And the viewers were no saints either.

TV cameras and news vans looked out of place in Fort Erie. Just seeing a neighbourhood she knew on the tube felt so strange to her.

She didn't know the family, but that didn't matter a damn. To think that a family should be brutally murdered was awful enough without matching names to faces. Rhonda Simmons finished by saying that the police haven't considered the crime scene to be a murder-suicide and that they were actively seeking a suspect outside of the home.

"Sure hope they find the guy," she whispered to herself. Then she clicked the TV off and went to sleep.

The next day, Thomas arrived right on schedule, with a new package in his hands. Maybe it would be a real gift this time, she thought. Not that the first package hadn't been thoughtful, but she hoped for something to place above her fireplace or some handy thing to use in the kitchen.

But first, he kissed her as always but seemed reserved, like she might take him again, right then and there, just like she'd done in Toronto. A guy like Thomas couldn't relinquish too much control, no matter the relationship. But that was okay. She'd had her fun and planned to let Thomas reclaim the reigns anyway.

"You look lovely as always." He tapped her nose.

"Do I? Do I really?"

"There's no reason why you shouldn't, my sweet."

"I barely slept a wink last night." She dropped onto the couch, elbows on her knees, hands over her face.

Thomas scooted up beside her and threw his arm over her shoulder. "Tell me what's wrong and I just might have a little something to fix it."

Remedies seemed all too easy for Thomas. First, she considered telling him about her fight with Troy, but it was barely a fight, and she hadn't cared anyway. As long as she had Thomas, she didn't give a damn about Troy.

"It's what I saw on the news last night." Now Trish felt like a girl telling her Dad about a nightmare over a cup of cocoa. "You ever see something really awful happen and wish you could do something about it? Like maybe you could travel back in time, step in and change history?"

"A Good Samaritan act in the truest sense." He grinned.

"I guess so. It's just that so many awful things happen in this world every day, some of them close to home even, and we don't even know about it. But it isn't just that. I wish I could bring that family back, but I'd love to make the killer pay. I dunno, maybe I'm just grateful that nothing bad has ever happened to me."

"Your desires are deeper than that, my love. I can see it in your eyes."

Trish stood up. "I dunno, maybe it's because my hands are tied. I'm helpless. I wish I could do something more, but I'm just an ordinary person, you know?"

Thomas' lips parted and then he paused. Then he glanced at the package, grabbed it, and passed it to her.

This package felt every bit as light as the first package he'd brought. Another device with a button, perhaps?

"Go ahead, open it." He smiled, hands on his hips; proud yet impatient.

Trish tore the wrapping, found another plain box, and peeled back the packaging tape. Inside, she found another device, only this one was a lever with a knob.

She lifted it out of the box and held it before her eyes. This was no ordinary device with a lever, she thought. The first device had certainly made a difference. But then maybe that'd been in her head and she'd been ready to take charge of her life with Troy. Endless possibilities drove her nuts. Either way, the device had been a talisman in its own right.

Thomas took the device, rested his finger on the lever, but didn't pull it.

"You want to end that hopelessness?" he asked. "You can do it. I know you can. You can be the change you want to see in the world. And all you have to do is pull this little lever."

Trish touched her fingertip to her lip. If pressing a button could give her the courage to overthrow Troy, then a lever should seem like child's play. Now the magic behind the device seemed unimportant.

"Congratulations," Thomas said. "Sleep soundly at night knowing you've made a difference in someone's life."

Then he tipped his head towards the stairs. Trish started at the bottom step and let him chase her.

* * *

Trish checked her watch. Two o'clock on the dot.

No Thomas.

Normally, he was the height of punctuality, a man you could set your watch by. And he'd never stood her up. But then how many guys would no-show if they knew they'd score a certain lay?

Still, she worried that he'd grown bored with her. Not that she hadn't made the effort, she thought. She'd tried taking a dominant role, if only to spice up their sex life, but that had yielded mixed results. The idea that she wasn't a priority to him and he didn't really love her crossed her mind too. She could've been one of many frustrated women who he'd rescued and pleasured sexually until his work was done. To him, she might've been a toy to discard when he'd tired of her.

God no, she thought. Then she rubbed her temples. Thomas *did* love her, he would arrive no matter what, and she refused to believe otherwise. And why not? She'd pulled the lever that was supposed to change her life. Nothing was supposed to go awry—or so Thomas had taught her—and she believed it. In the meantime, she braced herself for an agonizing wait.

Her eyelids felt like sandbags. If she could sleep, she figured she could pass the time, but she doubted if she could rest with this load on her mind. Her couch beckoned her in spite of herself. She fluffed two pillows, laid back, and fell into a sleep deep enough for a lucid dream.

Finally, a knock at the door yanked her from sleep. Her feet kicked out and she sat straight up.

A knock? When the hell did Thomas knock?

She hoped he didn't suddenly feel like a stranger who couldn't stroll into her house at his leisure. When Trish stood up, she worried how she looked. Her reflection in the fireplace mirror repulsed her. She hadn't taken the time to doll herself up for Thomas the way she normally would.

When she opened the door, she damn near lashed out at the caller. A dark-clothed, white-haired man (she later thought he looked like Phil Donahue) waited outside, book in hand. Trish sighed. She likened her frustration to someone waiting for a crucial e-mail only to find an ad for Viagra in their inbox. Then she noticed the white collar beneath his coat, and the book's gold-trimmed pages. When the remembered how she'd worried about Jehovah's Witnesses when she'd first opened the door to Thomas, she nearly laughed.

She decided that it wasn't funny, but that it was bound to happen, like it or not.

At first, she said nothing, and they shared an awkward moment at best. She'd grown up Catholic, and knew that respect for priests was crucial—horrible inconvenience or not—so she paused.

"I'm Father Seamus O'Reagan." Fog streamed from his mouth. "I'm pastor of St. Peter's on Central Avenue. Door's always open there. Won't you invite me in?"

"It'd help if I even know who you are." She pressed her palms flat on the doorframe.

The priest sighed and shook his head. "Shame. Terrible shame. I prayed it wouldn't come to this."

What the fuck does that mean? She thought.

He shoved one arm from the doorframe and pushed past her into the house. At first, Trish was speechless. Had this old codger really just grabbed her and stomped into her house? Oh yes, he certainly had. She resolved to kick his wrinkled old ass once she was good and ready to react.

She wound up to throw a punch, but O'Reagan ducked, clawed her face, and shoved her to the floor. Then he pounced on her before she realized her fist hadn't landed.

He leaned into her face and she turned her head. His breath stunk like sour milk.

"So tell me, Sweetheart: Just how long has this little love affair with Thomas been running?" He bared a row of crooked, yellow teeth. "I already know what you two do; I've been tracking you for a while. I just don't know how long it's been. And that's what you're gonna tell me. If I have to, I'll make you tell me for your own good!"

Whether he was a priest or not seemed unimportant now. She struggled against his grip, but felt helpless. Whoever the hell this guy was, he was aware of their entire relationship. Did Troy hire this guy to lay a guilt trip *and* a beating on her? A private detective would've been far less surprising, practical even, but a priest?

She tried again to break his grip, but couldn't budge him. This son of a bitch was strong for an old geezer, she thought. Then he snatched a handful of her hair and dragged her to her feet. Using nylon rope from his pocket, he bound her wrists, forced her out the door, and to his Cadillac.

Where was the bastard taking her? Her curiosity didn't stop her from pounding and kicking his seat, if only to make him miserable. For a moment, she believed that O'Reagan was the only truly evil person in the car. And then it dawned on her: had he gotten to Thomas first? She dreaded the thought in spite of it being the only logical explanation for his absence.

Trish was now willing to believe lots of things that would've seemed impossible before. For one, she had no trouble believing that O'Reagan could've overpowered Thomas. She believed that he could've overpowered Lou Ferrigno.

Finally, O'Reagan slammed on the brakes, and the missing seatbelt thrust Trish forward, short of smacking her face on the seat. He hauled her from the Cadillac by the arms, this time before St. Peter's Catholic Church. So he was telling the truth after all, she thought. He pushed her along towards the attached rectory.

She decided to do anything he demanded. Nothing was off-limits, so long as she could have Thomas back in her life, and they could be happy.

How could this be happening? She thought. She'd pushed the button and her life had improved. Then she'd pulled the lever, and her life should have become better still. She was to be in charge of her own destiny, and now she'd been robbed of that by a man of the cloth.

Inside the rectory, she found paintings of what she figured must be saints, and an array of crucifixes. Enough to nauseate her, in fact. The damn place was freezing too, though she wondered if it was just her.

O'Reagan pushed Trish upstairs, but she stumbled after the first few, and nearly burst into tears. He stayed on her until he could shove her into the bedroom and tackle her onto the bed. Then he tore her shirt down the middle and ripped her bra off. She still scooted back on the bed until she hit the wall, despite feeling trapped. She refused to quit on herself.

"I'd make this easier if I were you," he said. "We can expel the sin from your soul, so you can have a happy marriage very soon, knowing how to be a good and dutiful wife to your husband. But you must learn how to cooperate."

Then he dropped his pants and boxers to expose a stiff, uncircumcised dick. How this old man could achieve and sustain such a powerful erection at his age baffled her, but then so did all of his other feats.

His words reminded her of stories she'd heard on the news about pray-the-gay-away churches that would attempt to beat the homosexual demon out of a child. Trish figured that O'Reagan had the same plans to cure her infidelity. That, and she decided she would need a miracle to be believed.

He grabbed at her jeans, but she held fast to them as her last refuge. But he was too strong for her, ripped them off anyway, and discarded them. His nails tore down her thighs as he ripped her panties off. When he slid into her, she didn't feel the terse pleasure that Thomas brought. She didn't hold her breath, shut her eyes, and shudder with delight the moment he was the whole way in either. O'Reagan plunged into her all at once, with no regard to pleasure.

She screamed for help, whether anyone could hear her or not. Her fingernails clawed into the mattress, but that did nothing to relieve her pain, and none of the fear that enveloped her.

O'Reagan shot a hot stream of semen into her. He pulled out, yet he seemed fit for another round. His erection had barely wilted when he yanked his trousers up. He left the room, lights off, door closed, thermostat turned down, and she didn't budge until the morning light. Would Troy know she'd been kidnapped? She thought it was unlikely. After her Toronto trip, he would think she'd run off on another wild weekend.

She'd spent the night plotting her escape. He hadn't tied her down, hadn't locked her in, hadn't drugged her, yet she insisted that fleeing this place would be easier said than done. In the morning, she meant to search the house for something—anything—that would do the old bastard in.

But when she crawled out of bed, O'Reagan stood before her with nylon rope. There was no such thing as going home. He bound her hands and wrists again, dragged her to his Cadillac, and drove her to a place where everyone told her lies. A place she was in for her own good, they said.

A lie was a lie was a lie. But if anything, she was safe from Father O'Reagan.

* * *

Now

Trish stood at the window and watched the procession of yellow cabs pass on the street below. She'd felt devoured by the skyscrapers and sea of people since they'd arrived. Honking horns had kept her up last night, or so she told herself. That the bed was plush, and *The Helmsley New York* had seen to every detail, made the experience bearable. Now she listened to the shower spray in the bathroom, and waited.

The taps turned off and she heard Troy step out of the shower. Soon they would stroll through Central Park if she felt up to it. The tickets to see *Annie* on Broadway were not an option, up to it or not, Troy had said.

She glanced at the diamond ring on her finger and couldn't believe she'd gone through with it. She felt trapped. But since O'Reagan had shown up at her front door that winter afternoon, she'd learned to give in. She'd given in to her hospital stay (not trying to break free had been her version of giving in). And she'd walked down the aisle with Troy in spite of her doubts.

She heard the bathroom door swing open. The scent of shower gel filled her nostrils. Troy stood behind her, wrapped his arms around her waist, and kissed her neck. She backed away from him when he tried to kiss her lips, but he caught them anyway.

"No need to be so timid, Honey." He rubbed her shoulders. "Isn't this the perfect time to relax? It should be the trip of a lifetime for you."

"I know," she whispered.

"Then why do you keep staring out the window, looking so forlorn?"

She turned back to face him, but didn't answer.

She'd been mute about her kidnapping and rape. Not even Troy, or any doctor at the hospital had known, but she knew her pain was greater than her past. Thomas was out there somewhere. If she never learned what had happened to him, she knew she couldn't carry on. Even if he too had been kidnapped, tortured, murdered, at least she would have some sense of closure. She could dismiss the idea that he would come for her. Still, living with disappointment was not the philosophy Thomas had taught her.

She wouldn't utter a word of her pain now. Not unless she wanted to return to the hospital, or as she put it, the place where people told her lies. And she knew that Troy held all the cards and could make it happen.

Troy kissed her once more. "What would you say to a walk in the park?"

Trish met him with silence.

"Come on, Sweetie. We can sit by a pond, feed the birds, listen to saxophone players, watch jugglers, you name it. I'll grab your coat."

She almost blurted out *I don't want my fucking coat* but had learned to filter out almost anything emotive.

In the park, she sat as silent as she had been in the hotel room. Troy kept his arm wrapped around her, almost too tight, while they watched passersby, and she babbled about how much fun she ought to be having.

She would admit that the play changed her attitude somewhat. She even cracked a smile. But she knew she would never be truly happy in this life, with this man.

And so Troy quit trying. Not once more on their New York City honeymoon did he tell her what to do or how to have fun. He packed their suitcases, hailed a cab to J.F.K. to catch their flight to Buffalo, and barely spoke a word to her. Even on the plane, he'd only asked her if she wanted to finish his Sprite. Maybe he was only frustrated, she thought. Or he genuinely thought that her melancholy had ruined their honeymoon. She didn't care which. She only cared that he wouldn't force her back to that awful hospital.

Back home, Troy returned to the university, and seeing him waist deep in research and papers to mark seemed just as well. Being home all day had its perks since she needn't hide her longing from Thomas there. Living without him felt like losing a limb.

She'd read and heard her share of stories about people with Phantom Limb Syndrome, who felt like they still owned the arms and legs that they'd lost. Part of her felt like Thomas had never left her, and yet she could never overcome the disappointment that reality brings. Imagination seemed like a painful way to compensate, but she would cling to it if it helped her through the day.

Sometimes she lay on the couch and waited for him to arrive at two o'clock. Other times, she would engage in conversations with him, despite her words being devoured by thin air. That she would only do in the privacy of her own home lest anyone think she was crazy.

And then all the principles Thomas had taught her flooded back. He hadn't come into her life to make a weakling of her. He'd tried to make her strong. The time they'd spent together had been training, so to speak. And she had learned to become her own, strong person.

Each time she told herself that, O'Reagan's image flashed in her mind. She felt him inside her, violating her. She struggled to shake that image from her mind, but it seemed impossible.

Since she'd been home, new rules had applied. Chief among them was to forget her life before the hospital, to allow her a fresh start. And Troy—damn him to hell—wouldn't hear of any ifs, ands or buts. Friends (what few remained) told her how wonderful, understanding and tolerant Troy had been through the whole ordeal. If only they could have seen him on the flight home from New York, she always thought. But she told them it was true, and that she was one lucky gal, if only to humor them.

Any other man would have ditched her for someone else, she'd overheard Troy's mother saying. And she'd believed it too. That would have been fine and dandy with her, in fact, since it would have left her free to enjoy her relationship with Thomas. Commitment would have changed so much, she realized, but she had been prepared to do the work. Happiness was paramount to her.

If she couldn't be happy, then life wasn't worth living, she decided. She had never considered suicide, and didn't consider thoughts like these to be a threat either. In fact, she thought it meant quite the opposite. She would use them to rejuvenate her life.

Upstairs now, she prepared for a search. Lord knows what Troy might have done with her instruments of life. Before O'Reagan (or, "The Fat Old Fuck" as she liked to think of him) had shown up, she'd hidden the device with the button, and the device with the lever, deep in their closet. She figured Troy would grow wise to her and start to ask questions. He might have found them by now too, she thought. Would he have discarded or destroyed them?

A dig through the closet was all that would be needed to find her devices. She crawled over a hill of clothes-stuffed plastic bags, CDs, VHS tapes and other junk she should have thrown out, and found the devices right where she had left them. She had not used them in nearly a year, but she knew they would still work.

Which device was more important? she thought. The device with the button seemed to have reaped more benefit than the one with the lever. Either would have satisfied her. That she could overtake her own life, and not leave others in the driver's seat, was all that mattered to her.

She chose the device with the button and pictured Thomas. His grin was most memorable to her, at least when she excluded private things. Then she remembered how he made her feel. She could have anything she wanted in this world, anything at all, so long as she was willing to take control. And by God, she was.

Trish drew a deep breath, closed her eyes, and pressed the button.

* * *

Trish waited on the couch and stared at the clock. It was 1:45. She watched the hands reach for 1:50 and then 1:55. The pain never diminished, but she decided it would be worth it.

The moment the clock struck two, the hour song chimed, and she closed her eyes. When the song concluded, she listened closely, heard the knob click, and the door open. Thomas strolled into her living room unmarked, unharmed, and he grinned at her like no time had passed. Trish was ready to cry.

She stood straight up almost in salute. His smile set her at ease. When he approached, she grabbed his shirt, pulled him in close, and kissed him.

"What the hell ever happened to you?" she asked. "Where have you been? You're okay, aren't you? Did he get to you too?"

Just then, she realized how much she sounded like a doting mother, and refrained.

Thomas' face turned ashen. "I'm afraid so. I know I don't have the marks to show it, but I've spent the last year imprisoned by a priest named Father O'Reagan. I know you know the man."

"I fucking knew it! I'll kill the old fat fuck bastard! How did he get to you?"

Thomas slipped his coat off. "Never trust a man of the cloth, no matter what he says to you."

Trish nearly blurted out *yeah, no shit* to him, but she stopped herself. She still had nightmares about when O'Reagan had kidnapped, violated her and worse yet had stolen Thomas from her. But she meant to let Thomas tell his story sans interruption.

"He showed up at my door, just when I was leaving to see you," he said. "That's why I didn't show up. And it's why I haven't shown up since. First, he accused me of stealing another man's woman and defiling her. Then he spoke of you by name. He said I was killing my immortal soul. I tried not to laugh and then explained that we've been doing something quite consensual, quite pleasurable, and that there's nothing wrong with that.

"And so he lashed out at me," Thomas continued. "At first, I couldn't believe how strong the old man was. I should've been able to overpower him easily. But he beat me, tied me up, threw me in his car, and drove me to his church."

"Don't tell me he raped you too." Trish's hands covered her mouth.

Thomas smiled, shook his head. "He thought of a worse fate for me, if that's possible, Love. He threw me in a prison beneath the church and left me behind bars this whole time. Bread and water, darkness, cold. I know them all too well."

"He had a prison in the church?"

"Not an entire prison, just one cell where I was left to rot. Anyway, that's where I've spent every day and night, thinking about you. I wanted to escape, only I didn't know how, didn't know if I *could*. But then I heard you call for me."

The button, Trish thought. Pressing the button had summoned her love back to her, unmarked and healthy in spite of his trials.

Then Thomas said, "The call was like an angel sitting in my ear. When I heard it, I knew I had to break free. I had to find a way to escape if it killed me. And here I am now, standing before your beautiful eyes, and not a minute late."

She couldn't fight her smile back. Kidnapping and imprisonment had meant nothing to him. If she could count on only one person, it was Thomas.

"And now that we're back together," he took her in his arms, spun and dipped her, "we need to have a completely new beginning. But first . . . ."

Thomas eyed the stairs. Trish was game. She started at the bottom step and let him chase her upstairs to the bedroom, pinching her ass all the while, just like old times. Their clothes had shed before they hit the bed, and he kissed her lips and cupped her breasts with the same expert touch. Having Thomas back inside her was like reclaiming all she'd been missing. She was whole again. But when it ended, he didn't let her lay back and rejoice in the ecstasy. Those carefree days could well have been behind them.

Normally, Thomas liked to stroke her naked arm, whisper sweet-nothings in her ear, and prime her for round two. But she found him to be unusually silent now. He rolled out of bed, stepped into his pants, and tossed her discarded clothes to her.

"Come on, Love, we've not got all day," he said.

Trish shook her head in disbelief. Not only had he never rushed her before, he'd never been so blunt. But forget that, she thought. Having him back was most important.

"Where the hell are we going?" Trish asked.

"Anywhere but here. But not more questions, capice? You got those devices I gave you?"

Not the devices that had changed her life, she hoped, but she wasn't optimistic. She rolled out of bed, dug into her dresser drawer, and produced the devices. She was felt pained to watch them leave her fingers when she handed them over. Thomas only shrugged at them before he pitched them into the wastebasket.

"What are you doing?" Trish asked. "Those gifts were from *you*. They're special. If it wasn't for them, I wouldn't have taken control of my life, and I sure wouldn't have kept my sanity."

"Love, you can do all those things on your own, but you've got to learn how to take the bull by the horns. You can't look at your life over the last year and tell me you shouldn't do it."

"Don't you get it? I wish I *had* right along!"

"Then come with me."

Once she was dressed, he took her hand, led her downstairs, and wouldn't stop to lock the door. He held the car door open for her. Once inside, she guessed at where he would take her. Toronto? Montreal? New York? Boston?

The possibilities drove her crazy.

Any place where she could be with Thomas, and where Troy and Father O'Reagan didn't exist, sounded perfect. But, deep in her heart, she worried that no amount of running would evade them.

Thomas fired up the engine, and turned the corner at the end of her street, but didn't head for the highway. He didn't stop for gas, or to buy food and supplies to tide them over either.

Instead, he stopped before a redbrick house with a separate garage, a basketball net, an Intrepid in the driveway, and a white picket fence. Trish knew the place. She'd driven past it almost every day, and yet she had never looked long enough to notice any details, or to wonder who lived there.

Thomas killed the engine, and she waited for him to open her door.

"Come this way, Love," he said, "but be quiet about it."

Hand-in-hand, they snuck across the front lawn, and peeked in the window at a lean, bespectacled man whose dark hair receded at the temples. Trish judged him to be around thirty-five.

"You know what this man's deal is?" Thomas asked.

"Haven't got a clue."

"Killed his wife and kid. Well, first the wife. Happened almost accidentally. Bout or rage went too far then he decided he couldn't leave his kid with that information. Realized he had to do the boy in too."

A knot tightened in her stomach, and she realized how much she hated the man already. If she could do anything about it, to make it right, she would.

But how could Thomas know about it? She wondered. The man was home, free, and the authorities hadn't discovered the bodies. How could Thomas have claimed the inside track on the event, much less the motive?

Then Trish was captured by the man's ashen face. He fell into a recliner, dabbed his forehead with a towel, and chewed on his fingernails. Then he popped up and paced the room.

Thomas faced her. "What're you thinking, Love?"

She wouldn't tell him that his inside track worried her enough to consider some distance. But she couldn't tear herself from him after a year apart, and that her love was too deep to push him away.

"I bet you wish he could have his comeuppance," he said. "No trials, no jury, no technicalities, no prison that'll segregate him from the other inmates so he can sit in a cell and watch television. You want some true justice, so he can suffer the way his wife and son suffered."

Trish realized how badly she wanted to see justice served. If society wouldn't pull the trigger, she decided that someone must.

"Yeah." She smiled. "I think I would."

Thomas unsheathed a knife. "Then together, we can make it happen. Come with me, Love."

*　　*　　*

Inside the house, Trish tried to force the notion of dead bodies, guts, and pools of blood from her mind. Thomas led her by the hand, through the garage, and into the house, where they waited in silence for the bespectacled killer. He had paced his way into the kitchen where he switched the light on to find them waiting by the sink.

The man froze. Trish figured he had expected the cops and was shocked to find trespassers in his house instead.

"The fuck are you two doing in here?" His voice was a low growl.

"No need to worry about us," Thomas said. "You just need to worry about what you've done and where you're going."

Thomas raised the knife and the killer's eyes widened. Then he poised himself as if to dare Thomas to pounce. Thomas took the bait, leapt on him, but couldn't wrestle him to the floor immediately. The murderer gained a quick foothold and Trish covered her mouth. Thomas slashed the man's hand, which distracted him enough for Thomas to slug him, and tackle him by the stove.

When the knife struck the linoleum, Trish dashed to swipe it. Thomas landed several more punches until the killer's feet stopped kicking.

Thomas had broken out in sweat. "Got the knife, Love?"

"Got it."

"Now all I need you to do is end this man. The honor is all yours."

End this man, echoed in her ears.

Trish gazed down on at the killer's bloodied face and didn't know if she could go through with it. She wanted justice served, and to see him suffer, but she didn't know if she could be responsible for his death. For a moment, she understood how executioners must have felt.

"Make up your mind already, Love," Thomas said. "Can't hold him down like this forever."

"But I don't know how to do it . . . I've got a knife, but . . . ."

"Use your hands, Love. You can use them to make anything happen. Forget about the devices, *you're* the one who makes everything happen."

Trish doubted she had it in herself to do it, but she knew she must, or the killer would gain the upper hand on Thomas. How they had landed in this predicament she could barely recall, but she decided to do what it took to escape it. So she gripped the knife, gritted her teeth, and scored the blade along the man's throat.

A line of blood followed the blade, and a knot tightened in her stomach as she ground the tip in deep. The killer kicked, squirmed and gagged, but moments later went still. Whatever he had done to his wife and kid, he had received back tenfold, as far as she was concerned. But that didn't stop her trembling hands from dropping the knife, and wouldn't help her hold her tears back.

A cold, tingly feeling enveloped her. How she had brought herself to do this was a mystery to her. Thomas stepped off of the killer, and a spread-eagle corpse remained. The damage had been done at her hands, and as much as she reasoned that he had deserved it, she couldn't dam the flow of sobs.

Thomas held her, but not as closely as he normally would. Trish decided it was because he knew what was coming, and she would live with it. Whatever happened, she wanted Thomas by her side, and it would all be worth it.

"'kay Love, we can't stay here forever," he said. "A mess is a mess and we've got to get moving."

Trish hadn't tried to think logically, yet she realized that she had left her bloody fingerprints on the knife, and that Thomas must have left prints all over the floor. The cops would link she evidence to them so easily, she thought. And, even if they escaped the house, they would never truly elude the cops. She knew they wouldn't be together once they were caught either. Time to go for broke.

As they made for the door, Thomas clutched his chest. He backed up, slammed into the wall, slid to the floor, and gasped for air. Trish had never seen someone have a heart attack (except on television) and assumed that was what was happening to Thomas.

"Thomas?" she asked. "Thomas, are you all right?"

"Fine, Love. Just need to catch. My. Breath."

His assurance reminded her of Troy's promises when he refused to believe that something, anything, was wrong. But maybe this was only panic, she thought. After all, Thomas was far too young for a sudden heart attack.

Thomas pointed to the door, but Trish wouldn't believe that he wanted her to leave. What was more, she refused to leave him there.

"Go, Love." The life had drained from his voice. "Leave me here. I'll be fine. Just forget about me and save yourself."

"There's no way I can go back to where I was without you!" She said. "And what about where I'm going? It'll be far worse than the place where people tell me lies. I can't go there knowing you're here!"

Thomas' eyes fluttered. Trish dug into her pocket, produced her Blackberry, and dialled 9-1-1, but her fidgety fingers mashed the keys. She dialled again, and pressed send, but she couldn't put the call through. Her battery was almost charged full and yet the phone wouldn't function.

Thomas' chest rose and fell until it collapsed. And right then, Trish's world spiralled into a blur.

*   *   *

At the kitchen table, Troy blew the steam off of his coffee, and waited for Father O' Reagan to touch his. He hadn't accepted a dime for his help much less his caring and compassion, and Troy wished he could do something for the cleric. But he would certainly waive it off like he had every other offer.

"We've done as much as we can do," O' Reagan said. "It's over with now."

"Is it?" Troy asked. "Is it really?"

"We just have to hope that Trish knows how to make proper use of her free will, since I know it's what got her into this mess in the first place. But since neither of us can control her, it's out of our hands."

Troy gazed down at his mug and sighed.

He couldn't believe that Trish had suffered another attack and needed to be sent away again. Where that someplace would be this time was up in the air. Words like 'criminally insane' hooked him deep in the gut, mostly because he found them to be terribly inaccurate. On the surface, she might have seemed wild, malicious, but Trish knew he was nothing like that. The root of her behaviour was much deeper, he knew.

It amounted to the same for Troy. The love of his life was going to be locked away and never let out. They would never enjoy the love, companionship and life-long partnership that they had anticipated. Trish wasn't the woman he thought she was, but he hated to feel that way. He knew the woman she was before she was devoured by whatever the hell it was that had overtaken her. He looked to Father O' Reagan, and braced himself for the truth one more time.

"Pardon my language Father, but just what in the blasted fuck got into her?" Troy asked.

O' Reagan cracked a smile. "In the church, we try to avoid certain terms, these days at least. Not so much to be politically correct as to keep with the times, but I might as well be very honest with you and use some tough words. I thought I'd saved her with the first exorcism, and that she wanted to get better. She put up one heck of a fight, but I'm absolutely positive I exorcised the demon from her."

"But if you exorcised it, how the hell did it get back in?"

"Free will, my Son, just like I said." O' Reagan finally sipped his coffee. "A demon can just barge right in the first time if they want. But once a priest has given them the boot, so to speak, they're supposed to leave the victim alone. And I believed that's what would've happened if . . . . Well, let's just say a victim can always invite the demon to return."

But why the fuck would she want to invited the goddamn thing back in? The words almost escaped Troy's lips, but he calmed himself.

O' Reagan reached across the table, but didn't take Troy's hand. "I know this must be awfully difficult to understand, my Son. But demons can be as charming as the devil himself, and the person they've possessed often fall in love with them. In fact, the formerly possessed person might not know how they can live without the demon in their lives."

"And so she invited him back into her life . . . ."

O' Reagan nodded, but wouldn't make eye contact. "Sometimes we're not powerful enough to defeat the most potent demons on our own. And if I have regrets, it's that I didn't monitor her for signs of relapse."

The idea that Trish could have loved anyone else, human or not, struck him first, but not the hardest. Trish, the girl he had met in his freshman year and had fallen in love with instantly, had been ravaged by this demon for who knew how long, he thought. He hated himself for not having noticed the signs. His career would have waited, because his Trish and her well-being were paramount to him. If only he could have known that the demon was back, he could have saved her. And he could have saved the lives of those she had killed.

Though Trish had insisted that the man she had killed had been a cold-blooded murderer himself, the wife and child she had accused him of killing had returned home to find their house lined with police tape. The news vans that had surrounded their property showed up at Troy's house a few hours later.

"So, what options do I have now, Father?" Troy asked.

"You need to move on. There's nothing left to do for her, because she'll keep inviting this demon back into her life, time and again, like they're meant to be together."

Troy paused and stared down at his hands.

"Sorry to say it like that," O' Reagan said. "It's going to hurt, I know it will, but we have to work through pain to feel whole again."

"I understand, Father. And I will."

But the words: *like they're meant to be together* echoed in Troy's mind. He shook his head and sipped his coffee.

Ruins

He stands amid the rubble that was once Mine #5 and #6 and lets the whispers fill his ears. They taunt him, rattle and shake him until he wants to slap his hands over his ears. Except he knows that the whispers aren't there, can't be there, but no matter how often he tells himself that, he is not convinced.

His legs ache and the soles of his feet burn. The journey into town feels longer than normal. The old girl—he still likes to think of the town that way—is empty, the stores closed, houses vacant and everyone has escaped save for a handful of precious loyalists. He blinks at the sight, eyes the building at the end of the road and finds the lights on. He swallows, feels his throat dried out, and follows the light until it grows to be as large as the sun.

On the front stoop, he stares at the door and hesitates. *God, how I could use an ice cold brew*, he thinks. He imagines the foam on his lips and the ale trickling down his arid throat.

The neon open sign is as dead as the town, but he doesn't mind. His fingers curl around the doorknob and he turns it anyway then he listens to it creak slower and louder the wider it opens. His feet sound hollow on the wooden floor and the must of stale air fills his nostrils.

Forty years ago, he recalls, the place was named Duff's, a place that he and the boys had packed from wall to wall every night after work. The juke box relic still stands in the corner but hasn't sung a tune in decades. The tables and chairs all look like antiques. Of all the places in town to crumble, Duff's strikes him the hardest. And since he can feel it, he knows it can cause legitimate heartache.

A man stands inside with his back turned, buffing the tops of bar stools and the bar's top with a towel, perhaps in a vain attempt to return the joint to its former glory. His hair is full and dark and his frame looks wiry. The man might be thirty at the most, he decides.

He drags a stool up as the young man mouths the words 'We're closed' but he sits down anyway. Then he taps a cigarette from his pack, pokes it into his mouth, and scratches a match against his boot to light it.

The young man doesn't wag his finger, doesn't scold him or say that he can't smoke in the bar like every other place these days. He just grabs a bowl from behind the bar and slides it before him, so he can flick the ashes away with his thumbnail.

New in town partner? The young man asks.

Not hardly. Just makin' the long trip back.

Name's Joel. He sticks out a hand.

He grips Joel's hand, pumps it twice but makes no introduction.

The young man has an accent, Yankee for sure, but he cannot decide if he's from Boston or just a run of the mill New Englander.

Then Joel ducks his head into the refrigerator, reaches for a Pabst, pulls the tab and pounds it hard enough onto the bar to create a hollow thunking sound. He reels the brew in.

I been here before you were born, he tells Joel. Back in the day, this was the place to be. I'm not sayin' it was no New York City, but this entire strip out here was just a bustlin'! No one was richer than God, but everyone had somethin' and the place was prosperin'. Not like it is now.

But it'll get better, Joel says. People want to come here now; they want to make something of it again.

That's why I'm here, he almost says, but sips his beer instead. He knows why he made the journey but not why he bothered. He could land himself into even bigger trouble that way.

Some dead things should stay dead, he says. No use in trying to bring 'em back to life if that ain't what they want. And towns are the same way. Don't push your luck.

Economy's tougher than hell too, Joel says, but I've got some inheritance money. Lots of it, actually. I decided to pour it into this place, make it live again.

Joel spreads his hands across the bar like it's the hood of a brand new Porche.

Nice someone wants to help it relive the glory days, he says, but I'm tellin' ya there are some things best left alone. Not that I'm trying' to discourage a fine, hard workin' young man like yourself from running a business. The entrepreneurial spirit is what America's all about, ain't it?

Sounds like you know an awful lot about it, pal. Joel places another Pabst before him and swipes the empty away.

So maybe you'd like to tell me about it?

*   *   *

No matter what, Billy was determined not to cry. But the more pain that was inflicted upon him, the more the lump in his throat grew, until he felt like it would consume his wind pipe and cut off his air supply. He wouldn't let anyone see him devolve into a quivering mound of mush; that would give them all the ammunition they needed to laugh even more.

At 20, Billy had a wife and a baby girl, and had spent six months breaking his back in the mines. His hopes had been much higher, but once Angela had announced her pregnancy to him, he knew that marrying her and raising their daughter came first. And he meant to make sure little Abby wasn't raised in poverty. After a few years of this, he would quit the mine, they could move to another town for cushier work, and his family would still be comfortable. But for now, the mine was where he was, and there was nothing he wouldn't do for little Abby.

The work was arduous, the risk high and the dust was hell on his lungs. But that wasn't the worst of it. Rudolph and Sam—or Ruddy and Sammy as Billy liked to call them, though never to their faces—did more to create an unbearable work environment than the conditions did. Billy was sure that he didn't fit in with rest of the old hands either, but their torment was much milder. What Ruddy and Sammy dished out was worse hazing than a young fellow like Billy could expect in such a place. He knew that they meant to break him.

He'd stopped eating at work altogether after they'd tampered with his lunch pail. Sometimes it would go missing and other times he would open it up to find his sandwich and fruit buried beneath a dead rat's carcass. Most days he felt his stomach grumble from the late morning on, and he found himself scrambling to the fridge every twenty minutes or so when at home. Other days he felt light-headed, dizzy, and he wanted to report the two stooges to management, but he knew who carried the most clout and that his problem would only be compounded. And so he became determined to press on, and to bend but never break.

But earlier that day, Billy had been left alone in the mine when the lights suddenly died and the exit had been blocked. Billy screamed and hadn't realized that he could have a phobia until after. He swore that he was suffocating and plummeting into the darkest recesses of hell. As he clung to the image of Angela and Abby, all he could hear were his own screams. And then finally, he heard a cacophony of bellyful laughter.

"Look at that boy!" Sammy pointed and held his stomach while he laughed. "He done crapped his pants!"

"Sure ain't one of the smartest in the litter," Ruddy added.

Billy didn't bother to tell him that he hadn't crapped himself and that he was smarter than they would ever be because he was too busy trying to stop his chattering teeth.

After, the foreman strolled by, told the boys to break for lunch, and all but ignored Billy who'd been left in shreds. This time, he wanted to rat them out, but he reserved himself. Billy crawled up behind mine #5 and struck a match to light his cigarette. Smoking there was forbidden, but he didn't care anymore. They could fire him for all he cared. Thoughts of Angela and Abby forced him to reconsider his nonchalance, but they couldn't change his mind. He felt his stomach grumble and he realized he could take just so much more. A return prank would feel so satisfying, but he had no idea how to pull one off, and he knew that he, unlike Sammy and Ruddy, would get into trouble for doing it.

When he saw Sam, Ruddy and the rest file back into the mine, Billy stayed behind. He'd get reamed out right and proper for not getting back to work right away, and maybe they'd dock his pay check, but he again realized how little he cared. He struck a match to light a second cigarette then paused. He realized that the power to change his life was pinched between his thumb and forefinger. Sammy and Ruddy would never be able to make fun of him again.

As he stretched his arm out, the match smouldered and the stink of sulphur filled his nostrils. He decided to jerk his hand back but was stopped by a blast. The sound was dull at first, but was accompanied by the unmistakable noises of people screaming that cut through him like a rusty blade. He wanted to turn and run, but he was quickly enveloped by black and orange.

*   *   *

And so you see, he says, they say you can still hear those poor men screaming if you light a match near old mine #5 and #6. Don't have to take it from me though, that's just the legend around these parts.

Joe buffs the bar, smiles and winks. That's some story there, fella, he says.

Without the mines, this place wasn't nothin' but a bunch of buildings alongside a dirt road. They closed the mines up; people lost their jobs and had to move on. Town became as dead as those miners just that fast. And you can try and bring this town back to life all you darn well want, but death is permanent, and this town just ought to stay dead.

Joe shrugs and says, I wonder if that boy would even feel sorry for what he did if he could've lived to tell about it.

Surely he would! What do I owe you for the beer?

Three-fifty.

My God, what an expensive brew! He thinks. Then he digs into his pocket and produces the cash.

Thanks for the spooky story there, pal, Joel says. I'll be sure to keep my lights on tonight.

You do that there, fella. And don't forget what I told you.

He tips his hat to the young bartender as he hops off the bar stool and heads out the door.

He stares up the dirt road and worries that his feet aren't ready for a return trip, but he presses on until he reaches the mine. Pausing to survey the ruins once more, he scratches a match to light his cigarette, and hears the screams as shrill as the men's throats had once made them. They are close now. They come from within him.

Then he lays down in the dust to rest his bones, stares up at the sky, and is at peace. He is home now and he can sleep. And he finally realizes how sorry he truly is.

Open Doors, Closed Doors

Rosemary clenches her rosary when she stops before the door to the Tea for Two café on the corner of Central and Garrison. Her legs ache from the long trip.

The 'open' sign buzzes, and the awning is torn at the seams, but the inside is packed with people she used to know. These people pay her no mind now.

She checks her watch.

Have to get back soon, she thinks. One chance left and I can't blow it.

Have to get back.

She sucks in a breath of morning air and forced herself inside. A bell tinkles and Colbie Colliat's "Start at my Toes" is almost drowned out by the cacophony of voices. She stomps the snow off of her feet and everyone ignores her, just like she expects.

She sees a woman in a house dress sitting alone in the corner with her hands folded on the table. She isn't what Rosemary expects. There are no beads, funny-colored hair, candles or even a crystal ball.

Frozen at the empty chair that'd been pulled out for her, she doesn't move until she is told to sit.

I've been expecting you, the woman says.

Rosemary wants to know how she knows that she was coming. Does she know how far I've come? Rosemary wonders. She would spill every secret to this woman at her command.

Unsure what to say, Rosemary digs into her pocket for a wad of bills and peels off a twenty. Twenty dollars buys cans of Campbell's soup, Dempster's bread, Nielson milk and Crest toothpaste, she thinks. She checks her watch. Answers come at a price.

Have to get back.

Name's Elizabeth, the woman says. I have no control over your life. Please forgive me if what I'm about to tell you isn't what you want to hear.

Rosemary bites her lip as Elizabeth shuffles a deck of cards then slides them across the table. Tempted to push them away, Rosemary decides that she can't refuse the answers at her fingertips.

Elizabeth smiles and tells Rosemary to turn the first card.

Rosemary reveals The Chariot. Elizabeth turns over The Magician, The Tower, The Fool then sorts the rest in a square pattern. These pictures mean nothing to her and she refuses to believe them. Still . . . .

Life hasn't been easy for you, Elizabeth says. Not that it's all bad. You have Christ on your side but you still feel forgotten and discarded.

Rosemary squeezes her rosary until the beads leave marks on her palm.

You have two children, Elizabeth says.

No, I don't.

Yes, you do.

Listen to me, I don't have any children.

Want your answers or not?

Yes.

You have two boys.

Is that in the cards?

Your whole life is in these cards.

Then you know why I've come so far to see you?

No parent can be with their child every waking moment to make sure they're making the right choices. Most would kill to find out what their kids are hiding . . . some are just more intrusive than others.

Rosemary's hangs her head then forces herself to face Elizabeth.

You've had some terrible wrongs done to you, Elizabeth says.

It's not the boys' fault, Rosemary says. The lies they've been told about me . . . .

Ever hurt them?

Never . . . not intentionally. They've had so many problems and I just wanted to help them.

The older boy has attempted suicide, Elizabeth says.

Hail Mary, Full of Grace, the Lord is with thee, Rosemary whispers under her breath.

She wants to hold his hand, squeeze it tight, and stop him from destroying his life but she knows that she is powerless.

Isn't there any good news? Rosemary asks.

Believe it or not, Elizabeth says, you'll have the younger boy's love again.

Really?

Really.

Why not both of them?

I can only tell you what I know. The younger boy desperately wants your love but he's too confused right now to take the plunge. Believe me, he'll come around. Count on it.

When?

Not until the father's dead.

When Elizabeth gathers the cards, she folds her hands again.

Aren't you going to tell me more? Rosemary asks.

There's nothing left to say.

You can't just leave me like this . . . I've come all this way. What am I supposed to do?

Elizabeth's lips stay still.

Rosemary checks her watch.

Have to get back, she thinks.

After such a long trip, she knows that she must take care of business.

Have to get back.

*   *   *

Rosemary wanders up the steps to Peter's house. Let the dogs bark and the neighbors call the cops, she thinks.

Lava colored brick trims the house and a swing hangs in the corner of the porch. Charmed by Peter's taste, she finds an open door but the lights are out.

Inside, she switches the lights on and hopes to find Peter. Certainly he will recognize her, she decides. Time cannot fade features and she knows that she would recognize Peter anywhere.

The designs on Peter's wallpaper are prettier than the wallpaper and wooden paneling on her walls. The front door, the kitchen, closet and bathroom doors have all been left open. Rosemary stands on a hardwood floor and gazes at a plasma screen television sitting in the corner of the living room. A leather couch sits in front of the television and a love seat is just adjacent. Vanilla hanging in the air soothes her when an orange cat hurries past.

In the kitchen, she notices a sink full of dishes; some are caked with old spaghetti sauce and noodles, and others with mashed potato residue and broccoli grits. She scrapes the plates off, loads them into the dishwasher, adds a scoop of Cascade and fires the machine up. Some chores need finishing, she decides, and she doesn't mind doing them. The floor is clean enough to slip on, which pleases her. When she opens the refrigerator door, she finds a carton of soy milk, bottles of Poland Springs water, and a crisper loaded with broccoli, lettuce, carrots and tomatoes. Sliced chicken and turkey breast is the only meat she finds.

A magnetic calendar is posted on the fridge with red film smeared in the middle. Days at the beginning, middle and end of the month are circled in bright red. Business meetings are scheduled for the first and last Friday of the month and are circled in blue. A woman named Nadia's spinning classes are scribbled in with a fine black marker every Tuesday afternoon.

No wonder there's no time for doing dishes, Rosemary thinks.

A pad hangs next to the calendar where Peter and Nadia write notes to each other, in the streams of consciousness of an ongoing story. They end each message with 'love you' or xoxo.

Next, Rosemary explores the upstairs where she finds more open doors. She sneaks into the second door on the left and switches the light on. A king sized bed consumes the far half of the room and a television sits in the corner. Boxers, panties, socks and t-shirts are scattered about the floor. She gathers the clothes, piles them into a laundry basket then folds the bed sheets.

A picture of Peter, Nadia, she assumes, and a little girl with strawberry curls sits on the dresser. The girl looks to be about three years old and Rosemary wonders how much she's missed while she's been away. The family crouches before Cinderella's castle at Disneyland, wearing black mouse ears and smiles. More than anything, Rosemary wishes that she could hold the little girl in her lap. Just learning her name would make her happy. The calendar on the fridge has no dentist appointments or parent-teacher conferences and the house's open doors are driving her crazy.

Have to get back.

Back in the hall, Rosemary finds a closed door.

She turns the knob, and eases the door open, but not enough to stop a creaking sound. No one can hear her, she decides, but . . . . She switches the light on and nearly chokes. Inside, she finds a bed with posts shaped like school pencils and a dresser in the corner. Rosemary decides that a room like this is no place for a child to live.

Still, she decides that she must find some way to learn the girl's name. Answers.

She inches closer to the dresser, finds a picture of the girl on a swing, and figures that she's five or six in this one. She lifts the photo, and holds it close, but worries that she will smudge the glass.

In the top drawer, she finds several hospital bracelets with the name Mackenzie on them. Various ages are printed on them but they stop after age eight. Rosemary drops the bracelets and hurries out of the room.

Downstairs, she awaits the open door. Time is too short for her to care who will see her leaving

She has a long trip ahead of her.

*   *   *

Rosemary trudges through the snow, and is careful not to slip on the ice beneath. The night has grown silent and she clutches herself for warmth. Her legs ache and she worries that she cannot make the trip back, but she knows that she must. Her escape from Peter's house had been uneventful, as she moved swiftly out the front door, and was certain that no one had seen her, but still . . . .

Rosemary wishes that she hadn't sought out a single answer. This trip has brought her nothing but pain but Peter's happiness is all that matters to her. On the inside, she knows that he is suffering, just as Rosemary has suffered for years. His Mackenzie is lost and Rosemary is determined to find her.

She checks her watch. Have to get back.

The next life is no place for little girls, Rosemary thinks. Not her sweet Mackenzie. When she finds her, Rosemary is determined to throw her arm around her, and take good care of her, until her dear Peter can be with her again.

When she approaches the Anglican Church overlooking the Niagara River, she bursts through the cemetery gate, and weaves through the gravestones.

One stone sits alone, buried in snow, but Rosemary looks no farther. She dusts some snow off with her foot, but not enough to uncover the epitaph, and she is glad. At one point, a second stone would have accompanied it, but Rosemary finally understands that everything changes.

She lies in the snow, rests her aching legs, stares up at the sky, and shuts her eyes.

Roy sits out on Front Street each morning when the rush of traffic squeezes into Toronto and holds his tin cup out in case some generous soul digs into their pocket and tosses some change to a pitiful soul. Sometimes they do and sometimes they keep on walking. They're all stuffy, middle-aged men in handsome dark suits, cream white shirts and carefully knotted ties, who already look rankled from an hour or two on the Go Train.

Friday sits beside Roy from daybreak to evening rush, wearing a pressed suit and Gucci shoes, just like the businessmen who may or may not pay Roy any mind. When people toss Roy nickels and dimes, they seem to gloss over the well-heeled gentleman sitting beside him, perhaps because he's one of their own. While Roy sits on the cold concrete in his crusty parka, tattered jeans and sleeping bag rolled up next to him, Friday kicks his feet up and laces his fingers behind his head. Friday munches on a bagel from the Tim Horton's down the street and sometimes throws the last bite away while Roy prays that he's collected enough pity to afford a Hershey's chocolate bar.

Friday has shadowed Roy since his house in Mimico, where he has shelter, warmth, love and three meals each day. Men in tailored suits and deep grooves in their slicked hair suddenly appearing in one's life can be off-putting, but somehow Roy copes. Sometimes Friday's presence is inconvenient but Roy realizes that he has very little to say about it anyhow. Roy cannot tell Friday to get the hell out of his house before he calls the cops or pounds the shit out of him personally. It doesn't work quite that way.

Cassie and Amanda don't seem to mind having Friday around. In fact, they set an extra chair at the dinner table for him each night. Seeing Friday fork mashed potatoes and chicken into his mouth on

Mondays, spaghetti and meatballs on Wednesdays, and pizza and wings on Saturdays tells Roy that Friday is here to stay. Sometimes Cassie and Amanda say that they love Friday. Other times, they say that they would be happier if Friday lived with them forever and Roy hit the road.

Sometimes the creaking of bedsprings and sounds of giddy laughter from Roy's bedroom doesn't signal Friday to stay away, but Cassie doesn't seem to mind. Friday shows Roy how to love Cassie sweetly and skilfully.

When Roy stumbles through the front door on a frosty December night, Friday's arms are crossed, knowing where Roy has been. Friday has been with him the whole night buying him shot after shot. Friday drags Amanda out of the house kicking and screaming but it's okay because she's bruised anyway. Friday hauls Roy's little girl off to Neverland, and Roy believes there is plenty he can do about it, but then Friday reappears and it's too late.

Punishment is Friday's strong suit. Tough love isn't poignant enough for Friday, Roy thinks. That's okay. Friday is simply moulding Roy in his own image so he can live a better life.

Cassie tells Roy that if he could be more like Friday, their marriage would be perfect.

Roy assures Cassie that he has made some pitiful mistakes, but that he is a changed man, and he vows to be the perfect husband that Friday would be.

In the spring, Roy stumbles through the front door again, this time wearing greasy red smudges on his cheeks and lips. Before a fight can ensue, Friday carries Cassie out the back door and flies her away to a Neverland separate from Amanda.

Reflecting on those nights, Roy glances at Friday, awaiting an explanation, a promise to bring Amanda and Cassie back, but Friday simply stares at passersby, never speaking a word to them, and never speaking a word to Roy.

Roy borrows money from the safe at work and Friday makes sure that Mr. Harvey the bank manager doesn't see him. He plans to put it all back once his bills are paid up but there are far too many. Friday summons Mr. Harvey and Roy wants to say that Friday put him up to it but no one believes that Friday would do such a thing. Next thing Roy knows, his front door is locked and his car doesn't start.

Punishment is Friday's game. Roy thinks that if he can be more like Friday, Amanda and Cassie would still be with him, the name plate on the office door would still bear his name, and he wouldn't be living on Front Street. Except that Roy knows that he cannot change these things with Friday constantly on his back.

Glancing at Friday once more, Roy hopes that Friday will run into Union Station and buy him a coffee, a bagel, a cinnamon roll, a slice of pizza, anything, but he never does. Friday simply sits there, silent, waiting, calling on Roy to give in.

When Roy doesn't give in, Friday says nothing, and resumes his cold stare at the passersby. Roy wants to have Cassie and Amanda and his office back but he is determined to take his life back on his own terms.

Friday's slanted eyebrows and pursed lips tell Roy differently.

*   *   *

Roy finds his wallet on the slushy sidewalk. He dusts the crud off, opens it half way then slams it shut. Friday stares at him with trademark slanted eyebrows and pursed lips. No words, just a disapproving glare.

"I have to find out who this belongs to," Roy says but Friday doesn't budge.

Roy opens the wallet and finds a glossy Ontario driver's license with the crisp color photo of a man in his middle twenties. His jaw is cut square, his dark hair is cut short, and his doe-like eyes permeate the photo. His name is Christopher F Donnely and he lives on Younge Street.

That's just a block away, Roy thinks, though he realizes that the trek up Younge Street itself might be a long one. Roy hopes that returning the wallet to Donnelly will place him back in Friday's good graces. Every act of charity wipes out a multitude of sins, Roy thinks, and he hopes that Friday will bring Cassie and Amanda back. Roy decides not to ask Friday for a promise. Friday makes no guarantees.

Roy rifles through the crisp bills inside. Fives, tens, twenties. Mostly twenties. He finds more than enough money to keep him eating for weeks or to score a hotel room for the night. Nothing extravagant, he realizes, but any warm place to rest his head would please him.

Then Roy seals the wallet and realizes what he has to gain. He wants Amanda and Cassie back. Amanda and Cassie might be bruised and bloody, but Roy wants them back anyway. Friday might bring them back if her returns the wallet. Friday will never bring them back if he takes the money and chucks the empty wallet down the sewer.

Friday watches him, like a father, like God, making sure he doesn't swipe a single bill. Roy's hands freeze and his eyes stay focused on the street.

I'm no thief, Roy thinks, and he believes it too. Then he remembers the bank vault, and Mr. Harvey's eyes, and how his bank had foreclosed on his house, then his car.

With the wallet in clear view, he heads towards Younge Street, to Donnelly's apartment, with good old reliable Friday on his tail.

Friday wants to see the wallet before Roy returns it to Donnelly. Roy doesn't want to hand it over, but he knows better than to disobey Friday. Awful things happen when Friday is displeased. Friday peruses the wallet then hands it back.

At the front door to Donnelly's high rise, the security guard named Brandon snickers at Roy, but Roy can hardly tell through his sunglasses. I'm on an important mission, Roy says. It's a matter of life and death!

Brandon fights back a laugh and lets him pass through anyway.

Riding the elevator to the twelfth floor offers Roy the only sustained warmth that he has felt for days now. Music is something he seldom hears outside of the thumping of car stereos and now the crappy, tinny-sounding elevator music soothes him. Hearing Celine Dion reminds him of working in the office with the name plate that bore his name. He wants to hide in a dark corner of the high rise after he's returned the wallet but he knows that Friday will alert Brandon and that the cold sidewalk on Front Street will be the most that he can hope for.

Down the hall, Roy finds Donnelly's apartment. He knocks and waits. When the door swings open, the man with the short dark hair, square cut jaw, and doe-like eyes looked to be struck back by a pungent odour. Donnelly snatches the wallet out of Roy's hand. Saying thank you seemed to be beneath him and he opens the wallet to find it empty.

Donnelly asks Roy how he could be so stupid as to return an empty wallet and Roy insists that he didn't take anything. He looks to Friday for support but Friday glances away like he doesn't know him. Roy doesn't dare suggest that Friday stole the money. Not if he wants Friday to breathe life back into Cassie and Amanda.

* * *

Roy sits next to Friday on a long and cruddy bench. He wears orange coveralls with black, square numbers on the front and back but Friday still wears his tailored suit and Gucci loafers. Iron bars trap Roy in for the night but Friday is free to roam wherever he wants.

But he doesn't. Friday keeps close to Roy at all times.

When dinner comes, Roy sups on a tough slab of roast beef, lumpy mashed potatoes, and solid carrots, while Friday dines on a juicy steak, baked potato, steamed asparagus and a glass of red wine. Dessert of vanilla ice cream and chocolate fudge comes for Friday but Roy waits until morning to eat again.

Friday can leave before morning if he wants. Frank, the guard at the desk takes a shine to Friday, but Roy notices his angry stare each time he asks to use the washroom. Roy tells Friday to leave, to be gone, to never come back, but he knows that Friday wants to watch him suffer.

Morning comes and Roy returns to Front Street with his sleeping bag and cup. He tells Friday that he returned Donnelly's wallet, that he never stole a dime, and that he wants to have Amanda and Cassie back.

Right now.

Friday's lips still don't move and Roy knows that Friday will not breathe new life into Cassie and Amanda. Nothing Roy does can make Friday do that.

Roy begs, but Friday's look tells him that he has no remaining breath to give them. Wanting to cry, Roy decides to separate from Friday, no matter what the cost.

Wandering through Union Station, Roy waits until midnight, after the Raptors and Leafs crowds have cleared out. Mimico is the Go Train's second stop but Roy doesn't buy a ticket. Friday buys a ticket for himself and snickers at him. Guards sometimes prowl the platform to keep travelers from proceeding to the train early but the coast is clear tonight. Roy doesn't care anyway. There is nothing anyone can do to him now.

Waiting on the empty platform, Roy shouts at the end of the tunnel, and hears his own voice resonate in the night. No one will see him out here, he thinks, and if they do, there is little that anyone can do to stop him. Still, his choice is painfully clear.

Roy's toes inch over the chipped yellow paint but he doesn't care. Standing behind the line makes him feel no safer. Nothing anyone can do will stop him from doing what is necessary. Friday has to go. Roy knows that he must send Friday to another place, someplace far away.

Friday's hands are stuffed in his pocket, seeming immersed in the cool night air, when Roy notices a pinhead of light growing larger at the end of the tunnel. The train is coming he thinks, moving faster, stronger. The light grows larger. New life will be breathed into his lungs soon.

Consumed by blinding light, Roy shoves Friday past the chipped yellow line. Friday makes an *oof!* noise and Roy battles the undertow of gravity.

Two Little Dead Girls

Rain drums on the roof as Erica wakes, and when she opens her eyes and parts the blinds, she sees raindrops roll down the window like tears. She wants to stay in bed, but she knows that she must hit the washroom, then shower, brush her hair, dress, have breakfast, and ready herself for the day.

She hauls the bed sheet over herself, cocoons herself in its warmth, and gazes at the crease that runs down Michael's bare back. When he sleeps with his back to her, she takes a moment to admire him. Her fingers comb through his neck length, curly black hair, and she smells his musk. She sucks in a deep breath of his manly smell, holds it, and hates to leave him lying there. Mornings like these are always perfect to stay in bed together, and forget the world, she thinks.

She sneaks downstairs while still wet, and her hairbrush busy, but she feels refreshed from her quick shower. Quaker oatmeal with skim milk and only a sprinkle of brown sugar (her only vice) and a banana are her breakfast every morning now, as she is determined to keep the healthiest body possible. She understands that awful things will happen to her if she doesn't take care of herself. She sees it on television and in magazines every day. Lives become shortened and countless opportunities are lost because someone hasn't taken proper care of themselves. But she knows that she cannot live forever. She learned that at a very young age.

Spinning class will come after she's finished work, paid some bills, and picked up the groceries. Organic foods, vegetables, soy milk, and anything that she's read about in *Martha Stewart Living* are always the first on her grocery list. Michael eats most of it, but she knows that he sneaks the odd cheeseburger at work, or an order of wings and beer when he's out with the boys. Spinning class, Pilates and Tae Bo keep her spry, but she wishes that she could afford to take a day or two away, just to give her body a rest. Still, she is determined to maintain a healthy body so she can live her longest.

Erica loves the rain and gray summer mornings, so long as she stays dry. Michaels shakes his head when she tells him about her fondness for it, but he can keep his sunny afternoons, she decides. Inside, she reaches out the door for the newspaper and tries not to get wet, but she cannot avoid the sprinkle or warm raindrops on her wrist and arm. She stretches out as far as her arm will allow, snatches the folded newspaper tucked into the mailbox, and jerks it back into the house.

The newspaper spread on the table, she pinches her finger and thumb together to wipe away the newsprint that has already rubbed off on her. She pours herself a black coffee–-the only one that she will allow herself each day–-sits at the table, and starts at the sports page. The Bills first preseason game will be against the Lions and she wants tickets, but she knows that Michael will want to tailgate. Next, she reads the memorial page.

She realizes that she has forgotten all about Nadia.

Twenty years have passed since Erica and Nadia parted ways, but Erica realizes that Nadia is part of her, like the meat on her bones, and the blood rushing through her veins, and that they will never be apart. Twins have that inseparable bond, she knows, and she accepts that Nadia will be a part of her until her dying hour. But who placed the ad? she wonders. Mom and Dad are gone, and the death date wouldn't be significant to anyone else.

Erica throws her hands over her eyes and fights her tears back. Crying will do her no good, she realizes. She feels like an awful person, and a bad sister for forgetting, but she is desperate to put the past behind her. Despite Nadia's constant presence, she knows that it is the only way she can move on.

Rain pelts the asphalt as she sprints to the car, with her hand over her head, but she still gets wet. First, her doctor's appointment and then off to work. Waiting rooms always set her on edge, as she always expects to hear bad news. The clatter of children screaming and mothers yapping on their cell phones does little to calm her. Newspapers and magazines are spread out on the table, and discarded in the seats of vacant chairs. *Vogue, Time* and *Rolling Stone* are standards, but they never interest her. She reads the paperback that she brought with her, but she cannot focus on the lines, and soaks in none of the plot. The forty minutes that pass since her appointment time feel like hours, and she wants to stand up and march out, but she knows that it will not grab the doctor's attention. Rescheduling bad news is never easy. Doctors don't work that way, she realizes. She remembers how doctors can be so well.

Finally inside the doctor's office, she sits alone in a room at the end of the hall. Inside, she finds a scale, a sink, a blood pressure cuff, a box of latex gloves, and a poster that tells her what she can do to lower her cholesterol. None of the waiting room's personality exists here.

The doctor barges into the room and doesn't look at her. His eyes never lift from his clipboard and his glasses slide to the end of his nose. He wears a white lab coat with a blue dress shirt and tie beneath, not casual the way doctors have become. They exchange the normal empty pleasantries that make Erica burn inside. When he slouches in the chair next to her, he keeps to himself at first, but she isn't fooled. She always knows when bad news is on its way.

When she tells him not to wait a minute longer, and demands that he tell her the bad news, he doesn't hesitate to lay it on her. He is so cold and callused, she thinks. Maybe she only takes him that way? Michael always says that she overreacts, but she cannot help but feel tense when so much information is being withheld.

To Erica, there is no way to take what the doctor has said lightly. The disease that'd taken Nadia is alive and well within her. It chews at her insides, and pecks away at her little by little, as her flesh, organs and bones flake away to ash. The doctor says that she is not doing enough to help herself and that he can only do so much until she takes control.

How can you say that? She asks. I've done everything right, and this shouldn't be happening. The doctor does nothing to comfort her.

Even cold doctors can be politically correct, she decides, as the doctor uses diplomatic, professional language now, as if that can absolve his rudeness. A referral to every other doctor in the Niagara Region is one way of washing his hands of her, but she hasn't given up on him yet.

When he tells her that the illness was inevitable, he rests his hand on her shoulder, and says that he will do everything he can to help her fight it, but that he'll need her to be proactive. She can't believe that he would say that. Doctors aren't optimistic in her experience. She wants to storm out of his office, but she breaks down in tears instead. A meltdown in front of him means that he has won, and she won't let that happen, but it's too late.

On the drive home, Erica drifts off, as the wipers shove even heavier torrents of rain away, and he windshield fogs up. Pulling over and collecting herself sounds like a good idea. The past will vanish no sooner than her illness will, she decides. The doctor tells her to be proactive, but she loathes digging so far into the past.

She remembers Nadia's clammy touch and the antiseptic smell, the bed with bars on the sides, the stuffed animals, and how she's laid awake at night after visits. Sounds of Mom and Dad's fights are still fresh in her memory.

The house is empty when she returns home. The television switched on, she ignores its buzz as she scurries around the house, picking up junk, and putting the peanut butter jar that Michael has left on the counter back in the cupboard, and decides to shut it off. Any noise is too distracting now. Telling Michael about the cancer will be brutal, but she knows that he will be strong. If anyone can help her to take control of the problem, it's him. Michael is a rock and she knows that she can count on his support.

Erica stops in the middle of the living room and throws her hands over her face. For her, what's worse than anything is that she has forgotten everything that has ever happened, like she never had a sister, like the cancer hasn't been dormant in her body since childhood. Nadia has been a character who has only existed in people's stories, in their memories, and their darkest dreams.

Now if I could just turn back time, she thinks. She realizes that she will have to face the pain again. A childhood so rife with anguish will be awful to remember, but she knows that it's the only way to reconnect.

A trip back in time has never felt so vital to her.

*   *   *

The room has brown drapes and fuzzy orange chairs sit in each corner, holdovers from the 70s for sure, but everything else looks modern. Erica squirts a dollop of rubbing alcohol on her hands, and the smell strikes her sinuses before she can lather, the way it does in each visit to the hospital. Mom says that everyone must use it so they don't spread germs. Sometimes she, Mom and Dad wear green gowns, masks and caps in case of a flu outbreak. Erica wonders how germs can possibly spread with everyone wearing gowns and using rubbing alcohol.

For Erica, hospital visits are painful, but they have their perks. She gets to eat McDonalds and stay up way past her bedtime, but her eyes are heavy, and she feels cranky from listening to Mom and Dad fight all last night. Her pillows over her ears, she tries not to listen to them argue over what to do, or what to say, but that never works. That muffles the words, but the sounds still exist. She knows that they're talking about, and she won't believe it. Next come the tears, mostly from Mom, but sometimes Dad cries too. When they make up, Dad tells Mom that everything will be all right, and Erica hears them pray together. They've almost never gone to church, but Dad says that praying to anything that might help is welcome now. Erica doesn't believe him, but she clasps her hands at prayer time anyway.

When they pause before Nadia's room, the teddy bear tucked under Erica's arm is stripped away from her. She stands on her tiptoes, and tries to snatch it back, but Dad holds it over his head, and his expression never flinches. Inside the room, he hands the bear to Nadia, who is just waking now.

Unsure what is wrong with Nadia, Erica only knows that it will require heavy treatment, a great deal of love. Everyone sends Nadia gifts and candy, even people they don't know. No one gives Erica anything. Birthdays and Christmases come and go with a pittance if she's lucky. She is pushed into the shadows, she knows, but sometimes life and the people in it are plainer to see from the darkness.

Nadia forces a half-smile when Dad slides Erica's teddy bear under her arm. Erica stands at the foot of the bed and realizes how different this bed is from her Gem and the Holograms bed at home. There, she can hop in and out of bed at will, but not here. Erica also realizes that she is the mirror image of the sick girl with the hospital bracelet on her wrist. They share every feature, she realizes, and their voices sound alike. Except that she doesn't look like her anymore. Not with all the weight that she's lost. Her skin has turned tough, her hair is frazzled, and her voice sounds chapped. When Erica stares into Nadia's eyes, she knows that they are still one and the same and they always will be.

Erica remembers Mom's stories about how she and Nadia shared her womb, whatever that means, and that they share a body, mind and soul. With Nadia so sick, Erica worries that she will share their sickness too. Nadia's look tells her that poison is in their blood and that it will catch up with her. Maybe not today, but someday.

Dad combs his fingers through Nadia's hair and says: How's my big, strong girl doing today?

Nadia says: Doing all right. Hope I can come home soon.

Nadia sounds weak, and Erica knows that she's faking it. Always one to put on a show, Nadia snatches Mom and Dad's attention to herself every time.

Mom rushes to Nadia's side, just as Erica knew she would. You can come home real soon, she says, but you have to do what the doctors and nurses tell you, so you can get better. 'kay?

Nadia's mouth opens to speak but Dad stops her. He says: You've got to get better before you can come home. Not that we don't want you back with us. We've got your room ready, and all your toys are waiting for you, but we can't take any chances.

When Dad kisses Nadia on the head, Erica inches up to him, hoping that he'll kiss her, or hug her, or say that he loves her, but he only shoves her back without a glance.

Crying doesn't work. She's tried that. Whining and blubbering only makes Mom and Dad angrier until they tell her to suck it up like a big girl. There are more important things to worry about than her, they always say. Erica knows that she is stronger now than she ever was, but being a rock means little to her now that she must stifle her every emotion.

A nurse pushes a plastic cart into the room and Erica almost leaps out to hug her. The woman's name is Trudy, and she's wide with legs like tree trunks, but Erica doesn't mention her size now that Mom and Dad have yelled at her for doing that. But it's okay. Trudy laughs whenever Erica says anything that can get her into trouble and she makes visits to Nadia's room bearable.

When Trudy sorts her cart, she leans down and asks Erica if she wants something to drink. Erica always asks for apple juice. One tall one, coming your way, Trudy says. She pours Erica her juice in a real glass, not one of those dinky plastic cups with a handle that she gets at home. Trudy dips a straw into the drink, hands it to her, and pats her on the head. Just like her Nana, Trudy always knows how to make Erica feel better.

Trudy wraps a cuff around Nadia's arm and pumps a round, black ball in her hand, until the cuff inflates. Nadia stirs, but she calms when Trudy rests her hand on her forehead. She checks Nadia's temperature, and tells her that she may have something to drink now, but just a little bit. When Nadia fusses, Mom and Dad insist that she should be allowed to have more juice, but Trudy tells them that she would love to give her chocolate milkshakes, but she can't, and that it's doctor's orders.

Mom and Dad nod their heads, and pretend to understand, but Erica knows that they will badmouth Trudy the moment she leaves the room. Trudy pats Erica on the head once more before she hears the wheels on her cart turn.

While Erica sucks the juice through her straw, Erica stops when she notices that Nadia's eyebrows are slanted and her lips are pursed. This seems to sap what little strength is left in her body. Erica has the extra juice that Nadia wanted, and she won't let her forget it, but Erica tells herself that she is only imagining things.

Dad cups each of Nadia's hands in his and says: When you get better, and come home, you can have anything you want. Just tell me what that is, and your Mom and I will take care of it. It'll be waiting for you when you get better. I promise.

Nadia asks for nothing. She tells Dad that she would like to have her stuffed animals waiting for her when she comes home, and that she misses Mister Pilkington the most. Dad says that she'll have them all lined up on her bed like brave soldiers. Glad that Nadia asks for nothing more, Erica knows that it would be one more thing that Nadia would have that Erica wouldn't. Still, that dirty look hasn't left Nadia's face, and Erica knows that she has imagined nothing.

When she loses herself in that stare, the apple juice slips out of her hand, and shatters on the floor.

Erica chokes. Dad's hand flies and backhands her across the face. She feels nothing at first, but her sense of taste and smell vanish. When Dad jerks back, Mom rubs her cheek and says that he doesn't mean to be like that. Dad says nothing in his defense and even Mom seems unable to choke her own anger back.

She struggles not to cry, but she can't help herself this time. Tears roll down her cheeks, which will only make Dad angrier. He says that when he gets her home, that she will have plenty to cry about. She cringes at the thought, as she cannot believe that her night can get any worse.

Next, Dad says that he's so pissed that he can't stay in the room anymore, and that visiting hours are over anyway. He rips his coat off of the chair and throws it over his shoulders. When Erica glances up at Nadia, she checks for the animosity she was certain had been present a second ago.

When they leave, Erica decides that she doesn't care whether Nadia lives or dies. And she knows that the worst can become a reality. Mom and Dad whisper about it all the time even if they never use the word.

Erica hates herself for feeling this way. Even at her age, she knows how awful it is to wish that on anyone. Still, she knows that whatever lives inside of Nadia will live on inside of her just the same.

Her only hope is to break the connection, but she worries that she cannot save herself, and that no one will hear her scream.

* * *

For Erica, bad news is as hard to break as it is to relive the worst of her childhood, as hard as it is to learn of her cancer, and as hard as it was to roll out of bed this morning. The hours she has spent deciding how she will tell Michael doesn't seem long enough. She has considered dozens of scenarios, but nothing seems right. Sentences turned backwards, bent, broken then pieced back together do not seem adequate, tactful or sensitive enough.

Michael tucks a napkin into his dress shirt, which he never unbuttons until after supper, and slices into the medium rare steak that he's grilled on the barbecue. Pink in the middle, with fresh seasoning, the way Erica likes it. Gazing into Michael's eyes refreshes her, considering how she only saw his bare back this morning. She always takes a moment to admire the stubble that has filled in a little by suppertime. Tonight, this is simply a distraction. When he asks about her day, she bursts into tears.

Never one to handle crying people well, Michael stays still, like his seat is covered with crazy glue. He asks what's eating her, and she doesn't know if she should start with her cancer, or Nadia, or her entire life. Her fingers slide down her cheeks and she sees that he still hasn't moved.

First, she reminds him of the doctor's appointment that she mentioned over dinner last night. He nods and snaps his fingers. Then she says that her tests have come back, that the worst struck, and that she will undergo treatment soon. She says that she has cancer, and worries that something else is on the horizon, but then says that it's only cancer. First, he asks her if she will undergo chemo, radiation or surgery, and she says that she hasn't decided yet. Everything has happened so fast and she says that she needs time to think.

Michael tears the napkin from his collar, slides next to her, takes her hands in his, and tells her not to worry. Everything will be fine, he insists. She asks him if he believes that she's really sick then he pauses and stares at the floor. He cannot answer right away. She asks again and receives the same response.

She pops up in her chair like bread in a toaster, stomps out of the kitchen, and leaves her steak and baked potato almost untouched. Michael doesn't bother to chase her. If there's one thing that she's sure Michael knows, it's when he's stepped over the line and has really pissed her off. Normally she would count down the seconds until Michael delivers his canned apology, but she's too angry and hurt to bother.

Erica realizes something else: as long as she is married to Michael, she will give in to him, no matter the argument. Sometimes she wonders how Michael can cast such a spell on her. Mannerisms and subtle gestures are more powerful than words can ever be, she thinks.

Men with midnight black hair that curls at the shoulders, that have stubble that fills in a little by dinnertime, a crease that splits their pecks, and veins that squiggle through their biceps, can have their way with women, but Erica decides not to join them. As far as she is concerned, she is stronger than them. But when Michael strolls out of the bathroom in a towel, she wonders if the drops of water on his shoulders are still warm, and if his breath is still sweet despite the steak seasoning. She worries that she will fall deep into his clutches.

The towel still tight around his waist, Michael slides beneath the covers. Then the towel slides off and Erica knows what's coming next. She means to shove him away and tell him that she's too angry to do anything in bed with him besides sleeping, but he wraps his arms around her, and her fingertips run across his smooth, hot skin. She smells his Old Spice shower gel. Their lips brush against one another and she forgives him, just like he knew she would, just like she knew she would.

The mattress creaks as Michael crawls on top of her; Erica lets him do what he wants with her, sans argument. He tells her that she wants it as badly as she does and she agrees with him on some level. He always has been skilled. When his tongue snakes into her mouth, she realizes how much he tastes like cherry-flavored bubble gum. He spreads her legs, slides his prick into her and she wonders why holding her breath should intensify what already makes her shudder with ecstasy. When he finishes, he says that he's sorry for not believing her. She accepts his apology because she believes that she's sincere and because she's read about people who fall into denial when their loved ones become ill.

If she could help him to break those barriers down, she knows that Michael can continue to be the supportive husband that he's always been, and that her recovery will be much easier.

When Michael asks her what happened at the doctor's office, she says that she hardly remembers being there. An argument ensued, and she stormed out of the office, she remembers that much, but the rest of it is a blur. She's forgotten far too much lately, she thinks, and she never wants to forget anything again.

Michael tells her that humans forget sometimes. Erica figures that the brain miscues, a temporary information loss, but the data is still tucked away in some corner. Sometimes trauma makes you forget, she thinks. Your mind seals it away to protect you, but the memory has always existed, just as sure as the sun sets in the morning. Michael tells her that she might have experienced some trauma that makes her want to forget and that now is as good a time as any to deal with it.

Forgetting Nadia is unforgivable, she tells him. She has wiped her memory away almost entirely, not because she wants to, but because she knows it's for her own good. Deep down, she wants the connection to be broken.

Michael pauses, and just like at dinner, he cannot respond. She knows that he is smart enough to agree with or, or to avoid saying anything remotely flippant. Erica is sure of it. Disagreeing might work fine for now, because he's already gotten what he wanted, but there's still tomorrow night. Tomorrow night, Erica can play him like a fiddle.

When Erica asks Michael what he's thinking, Michael suggests that she reflect on the dawn of her adult life, and discard the rest. Worrying over the distant past, he says, is no path to recovery.

Erica tells Michael that he doesn't understand the severity of her cancer, or why Nadia's memory is so vital, because he never knew her. Sure, she's told him about Nadia, which is to say that she's mentioned her name. That is, she's told him that she had a twin sister. Nadia exists in a different life and Michael asks no questions.

Once she realizes what Nadia has missed out on, she can't fight the guilt. Nadia never knew how it feels to be an adult, she thinks, or to have a gorgeous husband, her own house, a career, a future and everything else that one only dreams of when they're young.

Michael tells her that she has enough to worry about and that she shouldn't torture herself. As far as she's concerned, she deserves the guilt, and deserves to feel empty, lost and depleted. No one who treats their sister the way she did deserves any mercy, in her opinion.

With an assurance that it was only childhood and that she likely acted on what she thought was right, Michael insists that Erica stow Nadia in the past, so she can focus on her recovery. Positive energy will reap positive results, or so Michael likes to say.

To forget is different than it is to push awful things away, she thinks. It's much different from the conscious effort to banish undesirable events from her memory. Since she has made that mistake once in her life, she's determined not to let it happen again. She owes Nadia that much, she figures.

Michael stays silent, like he still doesn't understand and, somehow, she doesn't expect him to. He hauls the sheets over himself and turns his back to her again, like this morning, the way he had before her life came to a halt, and she'd had to try and remember again. Before she can kiss him goodnight, she hears a muffled buzz from underneath the pillow.

Erica decides to close her eyes to try and get some sleep, but she knows where she will be once she drifts off. Memory has no barriers that she can think of.

Michael might believe that she can wipe away the past, she thinks, but he hasn't lived her life.

* * *

Erica doesn't hear the phone ring, but Mom and Dad's foot-stomps through the house eventually wake her. Mom rushes into her room, urges her to wake up and get dressed, because they've received 'the call'. Erica doesn't ask what that means. She goes along with it because she knows how fast Mom and Dad get mad when she doesn't. Another teddy bear is tucked under her arm, and she squeezes it lest it be stripped away from her. In the hall, she finds Dad with his shirt half-on, his hair frazzled, his face scruffy, and he is still in his bare feet. Erica rubs the gunk from her eyes and stares at him. He turns away from her.

As Erica steps into her shoes, Mom hands her some apple juice in a plastic cup with handles, and tells her to drink it down, because they have no time to spare. Her jacket hangs on one arm when they leave.

In the backseat of Dad's '83 Pontiac, she snaps her seatbelt on, and shuts up for the entire ride. Darkness shades the morning but grows brighter the closer they inch towards the hospital. Despite Mom's demeanor while dressing, no one speaks. Erica knows that

Dad will scream if either of them says a word. She is hungry but she won't ask for anything to eat. Food will come when it comes, she decides.

They dash into the hospital and Mom says that they should sanitize their hands first. Dad tells her to fuck the hand sanitizer and Mom doesn't argue. Erica has heard Dad say fuck tons of times before, but never on the fly. When Dad swears, Erica knows that he means business, even if it doesn't scare her. This time, the word hooks her in the gut, and she freezes. No way will she utter a word now.

They race down the hall that Erica has come to know intimately and Trudy meets them when they reach Nadia's room. Erica hasn't seen Trudy in ages it seems, so she leaps out to hug her, but Trudy pulls her aside. When Erica asks Trudy why she won't hug her back, she says that she doesn't have time to pat her on the head and give her a glass of apple juice. Even the ones who love you the most can hurt you, Erica thinks.

Dad scoots around her like a man butting in line, but Trudy doesn't falter. She tells him how sorry she is, but that they're too late. Had they arrived five minutes sooner, she says, they could have seen Nadia off. When Dad asks if Nadia had been alone, Trudy assures him that she was with her the entire time.

Dad pauses then slaps his forehead and Mom bursts into tears. Erica shuts up again, not because her wish has come true, but because she knows what Dad will do if she makes a peep.

Dad tucks Mom in close and asks if they can see Nadia one last time. When Trudy nods, and ushers them into the room, she reminds them that they must be quick, and that some calls will have to be made within the hour.

Dad's hand devours Erica's wrist. She follows him and Mom into the room and finds Nadia frozen in her bed.

At this moment, Erica is positive that she is still connected to Nadia, whose face has already changed to a cream color. They might not look alike anymore, she thinks, but they are identical at the core. Erica knows that their bond will stay intact, even if she wants to break the connection. At the very least, she has a message for her. She wants to tell her that she is sorry that she hated her, and sorry that she wished this on her. That Nadia cannot hear her intensifies the pain.

When they leave, Trudy returns with a sheet and covers Nadia, but Erica doesn't feel distanced from her sister. Dad wraps his arm around Mom, but Erica cannot bring herself to cry.

Two days later, Erica waits in a shaded room with plush couches, and decked with assorted colors, but she's hungry and her legs ache from standing around for hours. The flower fragrance fills her nose, and makes her cough, but she deals with that. Everyone, including faces that she's never seen before, shake her hand, and pat her on the head (albeit without Trudy's tenderness).

Mom insists on a final viewing before the casket is closed, and Dad tells her that he doesn't understand why. Always one to agonize over detail, Erica thinks, Mom says that she wants to make sure Nadia is positioned properly. They're paying the funeral home people good money. Dad tells her that the casket will be closed anyway, that no one will see her, and that they sure as hell won't see her underground, but Mom doesn't budge.

She says that she will know, and that will be hard enough.

Erica hopes that she never thinks like Mom.

While Erica knows what is happening, she struggles to inch into the church the next day. She forces herself past the black Cadillac parked at the back door, and down the hall to the sanctuary. The casket sits before the knave, with a linen cloth draped over it. Everyone asks her how she's doing, and she says that she's fine, but they insist that she doesn't understand what has happened. Why don't they believe that I'll be fine? She wonders. They tell her that one day, when she truly understands what has happened, that she will mourn.

To her, that means that she will cry, which sounds helpful, but she doubts that the tears will ever come.

By the graveside, everyone crowds around her, and she can barely see what's going on. She squeezes past a few people to get a closer look. The priest spreads a dust cross over the casket, bows his head in prayer, and then everyone scatters off their separate ways.

After the burial, everyone sits around in the parish hall and drinks coffee and eats finger foods prepared by the Anglican Church Women, and Erica again feels pushed into the shadows.

Sometimes it's nice here, she thinks.

The house is still cluttered with flowers and sympathy cards when they return home. The kitchen counter and dining room are cluttered with dirty dishes and mail. Laundry hasn't been done in days. Mom and Dad still have a few more days off from work, and Erica knows that she won't be going back to school yet. Those are some perks of the situation, but she realizes that it doesn't outweigh the drawbacks. She knows that she must think about what she has wished for, and how she will have to live with her guilt.

Once they finish their Chinese takeout, Erica asks if she can go to her friend Mallory's house for a few hours, and Dad tells her no. Now isn't the time to be playing, he says. Mom steps in, takes Dad's hand, and says that Erica needs to do something for fun, to forget about the weight of the world for a while. She says that is sending her to Mallory's house will help her, she's all for it.

Dad's eyebrows slant, and Mom shuts up. He tells Erica that she must go to bed this minute and that he doesn't want an argument. Mom doesn't step in to defend her this time.

Still light out, Erica stomps upstairs, slams the bedroom door, and shuts the lights off. She hears Dad's footsteps pound the stairs and she hears the door lock.

Worried that she'll be trapped forever, Erica lunges for the door, and know that she's trapped in her room at least for the night. She knows that Dad didn't do this because he loved Nadia more, or because he is so racked with grief. Mom and Dad hate her, she thinks. Maybe not Mom, but Dad does.

Had Nadia lived, it wouldn't be so bad, she is sure.

Unable to think, Erica stares at the wall, and shivers. She has until morning to figure out a plan, but she knows she is helpless. She can head out on her own, but even she knows that she won't make it past the end of the street.

Nadia might be gone, but Erica knows that no connection has been broken. Nadia could unlock the door and free her if she wants to. Erica wants her back, if only so she can tell her how sorry she is for wishing her dead. To her, she could as easily have been the girl in the box, and in the ground. She knows that what flowed through Nadia's veins flows through hers, and she is grateful for what she has left.

Erica slips into her pajamas, hops onto the bed, and holds her bear close. She decides to switch the light on, even if it gets her in trouble come morning, and closes her eyes. Before she drifts off, she prays that the worst won't come.

*   *   *

When Erica wakes, she is consumed by a darkness that reminds her of her childhood bedroom. She remembers having been locked in that room until the following dawn, how hungry and lonely she'd been, and how tired her eyes and muscles were from hours of crying. Most of all, she remembers how her father barely spoke a word to her in the months and years that followed. Mom isn't much more talkative and she knows that is from more than Dad's prodding.

Life is different now. Erica has a husband who listens to her and friends who reassure her. Raindrops sprinkle the rooftop and snoring noises buzz from Michael. Footsteps echo outside her bedroom door. Someone is in the house. Someone is in the hall.

Erica always shuts the bedroom door, but when her eyes open, she realizes that the door has been left open. When she sits up, she finds Nadia filling the empty space, frozen. Staring. Her doe-like eyes permeate her and she freezes and pulls the covers up.

How Nadia snuck into the house has Erica curious. She is drenched, but Erica doubts that the light rain outside could've soaked her so. To her, Nadia looks like she has walked through a deluge. The idea that she might've crawled up through the toilet has Erica ready to laugh, but she doesn't dare. She won't do anything until she knows what her sister wants.

This Nadia isn't like the girl she remembers lying in the hospital bed, hooked up to tubes and wires. To Erica, she looks more liked the healthy girl who lived in the bedroom next to hers, the girl that she knew from the womb, even if her expression seems vacant and bland.

She turns to Michael and realized that he's still sleeping, and doesn't see anything that's going on. She wants to wake him, and tell him that they have a visitor, but she worries that Nadia can suspend time and space. Whatever happens will be between her and Nadia, she is certain.

You're not here, Erica whispers to Nadia, but she doesn't hear the ghost of her own voice. She feels like she is trapped in a silent, black and white movie, and doesn't know what will happen next.

Nadia inches closer, floats across the carpet, and Erica knows she has a purpose. She wishes that she had slammed the door before Nadia could have started, but she knows that she would wait in the hall crying, scratching at the door, like a cat wanting to come in. The determined always get their way, she decides.

When Nadia reaches the bed, Erica sits up straight, and wants to scoot backwards. Nadia remains still. To Erica, she looks out of place in her bedroom, and in her life, as she knows that this life is the one that she was never supposed to realize. In this life, she is little more than a memory.

What are you doing here? Erica asks her, and this time she feels the words travel through her windpipe, through her throat and past her lips.

For the first time, Erica realizes that she can right her wrongs. She has the second chance that she has longed for. She remembers the day that she wished Nadia dead, how she'd scolded herself for thinking something so awful, and she remembers how badly she wanted to take it back.

Now that Nadia has returned, she can take it back, she can love her, she can help her to become well again, and she can finally have her forgiveness.

You can hear me, can't you? Erica asks. She knows that she must dig deeper to know if Nadia can truly hear her. If she can, she longs to pour her heart out to her sister, and to explain why she thought such awful things.

If she's in a forgiving mood, Erica thinks.

Listen to me very carefully, Erica says. When we were little, you were very sick, only you probably didn't know how bad it was. Probably didn't think it was any worse than a really long flu. A kid can't know those things. But I did. I really did. I knew exactly what was going to happen to you . . . and I wanted it to happen.

Nadia flinches, and then her head tilts like an inquisitive pup.

I wanted the worst to happen to you except . . . I never meant it. I never really felt that way. I know that sisters can do some awful things to each other, and I thought some nasty things about you, but I loved you every moment. I'd do it differently if I could do it over. You understand, don't you?

Nadia raises her finger, and Erica cringes, until she realizes that Nadia doesn't mean to hurt her. She stands at the foot of the bed, not smiling, but with a still expression, as she awaits contact from her sister again. That's all she can possibly want, Erica decides. Erica holds the sheet up against her chest, leans forward, and presses her finger against Nadia's.

If anything can prove to her that she isn't dreaming, the contact with Nadia's flesh will be plenty to do with that. Her skin is cold, wet and clammy, but Erica doesn't jerk back. Erica savors her touch, like she's cuddled up with a warm companion.

You're here for a reason, aren't you? Erica asks. Want to talk about something?

It flows through your veins, Nadia says.

Erica expects Nadia's voice to sound cracked, rusty and old, and is surprised by her crisp pitch. To her, it's clear yet very gentle, like a whisper.

And yet, she knows exactly what it means. She knows that what afflicted Nadia as a child now flows through her veins. Erica waits for the sickness to eat away at her blood vessels, to chew on her muscles, and to tear her apart from inside until there is nothing left.

Nadia grins and bears her set of yellow teeth, the same hue of yellow as her skin was when she was in the hospital. She turns and floats back out into the hall, which turns darker from her presence, and she becomes one with the shadows.

A soundless exit, Erica expects some loud clanging noise to announce Nadia's departure, or a splashing sound if she dives into the toilet bowl, but she hears nothing. This seems unusual to her, but she realizes that such things aren't meant to make sense. Still, she can't help but agonize over it.

It flows through my veins, she thinks, and forces a breath out. And she knows that Nadia's fate is her destiny. Bad karma aside, Nadia has a genetic curse that has followed Erica for years, and has caught up with her. Nadia hasn't delivered a spiteful message, she thinks, but rather is warning her sister.

If there's time enough to stop it.

Erica wonders if the cancer has been dormant in her since Nadia was ill. She figures that she could just as easily have been the one in the hospital bed twenty years ago, and could have been the one underground. But her time to die could be fast approaching, she realizes and she covers her eyes.

If another interpretation exists, Erica decides she will snap at it. She supposes that Nadia's ghost on her tail could be what she really means. The very fact that she cannot break her connection with Nadia, and that her sister is stalking her adult life, could be what flows through her veins, she thinks. This curse seems unbreakable.

At the very least, she knows that she must break the connection if she wants to be at peace. But how? she wonders. Tomorrow, she decides that she will lock the door, and take every measure necessary to keep Nadia out.

Michael still snores.

Erica wants to tell him about what has happened, but he hasn't budged throughout the entire experience. He might never believe that anyone was in their bedroom tonight. All a product of bad dreams, Michael likes to say. Erica wants to check the hall for evidence of Nadia's visit, but she decides to wait until morning.

Dear God, she thinks. Don't let me be right about this.

*   *   *

Erica jams a chair beneath the door knob, tests it, but pulls the chair out and decides that she cannot lock Nadia out this way. She doesn't want to entirely. Besides, she knows that Nadia will find a tricky way to wiggle out of it. The dead will persevere, she thinks, and decides that she should lock the door from the inside. Michael's tools are scattered on the floor around her. Some she doesn't know the name of and others she doesn't know how to use. She grabs a hammer and raises it, but doesn't know what the hell to do with it, so she drops it.

She checks her watch, and realizes that she should be driving up the QEW for treatment in Hamilton right now, but she knows that she cannot go anywhere with this load on her mind. After what she saw last night, she can do little of anything. She leans forward with her legs crossed and takes a deep breath.

A ghost was in her room. Though she needed hours to realize it, she is absolutely sure that Nadia is stalking her. Still, some shred of doubt remains. Sure, she made physical contact with Nadia, but she decides that it doesn't make her real. Michael surely should have woken from the noise and found the dead girl at the foot of his bed. But if she's real, Erica knows that she must break any connection that Nadia is trying to continue, and pray for the power to do so.

The dresser is her next option, but she knows that it's going to be a heavy bugger. She crouches behind it, shoves all of her weight against its side, but it barely budges. The carpet keeps her from pushing it in front of the door, but of course, she realizes that a dresser parked before the door is unlikely to stop Nadia from making her presence known. She arrived in silence last night, in spite of the locked doors and windows, and Erica knows that she will show again tonight if she wants to.

Part of her hopes that Nadia will show up tonight. Though it seems weird to her, she wants to continue her connection to her sister. Sometimes people want what's bad for them, she realizes, but those things make them feel good. They pull the downtrodden through the day sometimes. But she also doesn't like the idea of playing with fire. If Nadia returns tonight, Erica decides that she must fight the urge to take Nadia in with open arms.

She realizes that they can have tea parties, makeup parties, and the pillow talks that they missed out on as children. Even the hate and angst that she felt can now be washed away.

Except that she knows that some wounds aren't meant to be healed, and that she still hasn't figured out what Nadia wants.

Now, to find a smarter way to block Nadia out, she thinks.

Michael returns home from the gym, his hair slick and his body smells fresh from the shower. He knots his tie and stuffs his hands in his pockets. He always heads straight to work from the gym, but he says that he has forgotten his Blackberry on the kitchen table, and that he can't survive the day without it.

When she sees him draw closer, she grabs at his tools, even if she knows that she's too late to hide them. She squats on the floor, and slides the hammer and screwdriver under her leg, like a chicken on an egg. Michael's eyes slant, but he says nothing.

What are you doing here? He asks. You're supposed to be in Hamilton for your first round of treatments, aren't you?

Eleven o' clock actually, she says, plenty of time. But I'm not going. Not today anyway, maybe next time? Yes, I know how important it is, but I have more important things to do right now.

Michael takes her hands, helps her to her feet, and tucks her in close. Though she loves being pressed against his body, she can't help but dwell on the hammer, the screwdriver, the chair that she jammed underneath the doorknob, and how she will avoid her sister tonight.

Nothing can be more important than your treatment, he says. If you want to get better then you need to be there. Besides, what are they going to say when you don't show up? They'll drop you to the bottom of the list, they'll refuse to treat you, they'll . . . .

You can't worry about that, she says. Life's too short to worry about little things like appointments and lists. I know it's important that I be treated, but I also have everything in perspective. Trust me, Sweetie.

Michael seems lost for words, and Erica no longer cares what he will say. To her, everything is figured out and she hopes that he will trust her.

Please, Michael says. People get cold feet sometimes, and that's okay, but you really do need to go for treatment. If you're scared then you really shouldn't worry about a thing. I love you and I'll see you through everything. But whatever you do, please don't sit there and let this eat at you.

To her, Michael sounds like he is falling into denial again. She knows that he wants to pretend like there is something more at issue, despite what he has said before. Somehow, he still wants her to receive treatment, like he had never expressed a single sound about her sickness.

She wants to tell him all about how Nadia appeared in their bedroom last night. Wouldn't it be a hoot to meet the sister in law that you've never known? she wants to ask. But poor Michael, she thinks. He cannot believe in anything he cannot see or touch. So unfortunate.

You can always hurry off to work and let me worry about me, she says.

He pauses first, but she insists so he throws his hands up and shrugs. He kisses her lips and she rests her head against his chest, before she pushes him along on his way.

Then you promise you'll go for your next treatment? he asks.

She hooks her pinkie finger around his and says, I absolutely swear that I will. Now you get back to work before you're late, you crazy thing.

A peck on the cheek sets him in motion and she returns to her work. She has almost forgotten the hammer and screwdriver.

Part of her wants to welcome her sister home with open arms, even though she knows that it will not be good for her.

First, she lifts the hammer again, and searches for anything she can nail to the door to keep Nadia out. Surely Michael will think that she's being silly or overcautious, she thinks. She wants to come clean, but she can imagine his reaction already.

When she checks her watch, she knows that she will be late for her first round of treatments, but she knows that the only cure will be to break her connection to Nadia. The how, the why, and the when are meaningless to her, but she is positive of what the answer is. Even the struggle to lock her out seems silly to her, as she knows that Nadia will find a way in. Still, she knows that she must do whatever possible to block her out.

Break the connection, she urges herself.

It flows through your veins, she remembers Nadia saying.

What flowed through Nadia's veins now flows through Erica's veins, she knows. Nadia's body pulsed with cancer, and she knows that she now pulses with the very same cancer. Though the disease has taken several decades to catch up with her, it has no plans to elude her. Time to prepare for the worst, she tells herself.

She pops into the guest bedroom and grabs another chair, a footstool, and everything else she can think of to stuff in the front hallway. Nothing is too small, she decides. This way, she can slow Nadia down, if not stop her entirely.

Anything necessary to break the connection, she decides. But she fears that even running away won't be enough.

*   *   *

Erica tosses and turns but she is sure that she has fallen asleep at some point. Those moments when she slips in and out of consciousness, thinks silly things, and hears odd noises and voices, tell her that. Michael lays face down in the pillow, which muffles his buzzing noises. Like always, she thinks, the roof could collapse, and Michael would keep on sleeping.

She reflects on Michael's expression when he returned home at supper time, interrupted her work, and asked her what she's doing still on the floor with his tools. She told him that she is simply preparing for the worst, and nothing more. No need to be alarmed, she said. She never believes that the worst can really happen, but she said that they keep emergency preparedness kits, bottled water, and non-perishables, for an emergency that hasn't happened, and probably never will. Why not this? she asked. Though he only shook his head, the suggestion got him off her back for now. Unless he's been on to her the entire time, she thinks.

The dresser, a chair, and the piano stool sit before the door, but Erica knows that heavy objects mean nothing. Part of her feels lucky that Michael goes along with it. No doubt he figures her for a complete loony, she decides, but she knows that explaining to him that her twenty years dead sister could drop by any time will be far from simple. Making him understand that the connection must be broken come hell or high water will be an even greater chore. Still, she knows that she must try.

When she drifts off again, she hears a pitter-patter on the roof, but she swears that it's not raining out. She opens her eyes, sits up, and the noise persists. Her fingers open the blinds, and she sees no raindrops roll down the window. The door swings open despite all the junk she left in front of it and Nadia stands before her. Erica thinks she looks stoic, just like last night. This time, Erica doesn't back away, but she still refuses to take her sister on. Nadia's hair looks smoother than it had last night, and her clothes aren't torn or disheveled. Erica is sure that her cheeks are rosier than they had been last night.

She won't hurt you, Erica tells herself. She'll touch you, but she can't hurt you.

This time, Erica wants to wake Michael, so he can see Nadia, and so she'll never have to prove anything if he calls her crazy. Then again, she knows that he'll never understand what Nadia really is, and she can't begin to explain it. And if that happens . . . .

Nadia inches forward, just like last night, and Erica stays still. When Erica tries to speak, Nadia presses her fingers to her lips, shushes her, and motions towards Michael. Erica worries that Nadia can read her mind.

I don't know why you're here, Erica says, and I don't know what you want from me. I knew you'd get past everything I stacked in front of the door, so please don't think I was trying to fool you. But I can't go on being sick like this and it was all I could do to get better. I need you to leave me alone so I can live. Please.

Nadia stays quiet, but Erica is positive that her words have penetrated her.

If you're alive again, Erica says, then you must want something from me. Just tell me what it is and quit driving me crazy.

I can come back from the dead, Nadia says. You and I both know it.

But you're already here in the flesh, Erica says. I touched you just last night.

Erica leans forward to touch her sister's finger again. It feels warmer and softer than it had last night. Then she says: If I can touch you then you've got to be alive.

I want to live again, Nadia says, and I'm going to, no matter what. But I need you to help me.

Yes Nadia, Erica says. Anything.

The only way I can live again is if you come to the cemetery. You stood by me during my worst living moments, and now you must visit our grave, to be with me, and to give me my connection back to the living.

Break the connection, Erica thinks, you've gotta break the connection, but she knows that it will be impossible.

You're saying that you really want me to come to the cemetery? Erica asks. If I come, and I'm not saying that I will, what will I have to do?

Oh, you know you're going to come, Nadia says. Sweet that you think you have a choice in the matter.

And Erica believes her. She realizes what she must do once she reaches the cemetery. She must search for the double plot that Mom and Dad bought for both of them (as if they have awaited her death for years, she thinks). That and she knows that she may have to dig her sister's body from the earth. A shovel has been the one untouched tool in the garage, but what the hell, she tells herself. Sure, Nadia has said nothing of unearthing her remains, but Erica knows that it's coming. You can't have a scene like this one without taking on some gruesome chore, she tells herself.

Tomorrow night, Nadia says. I won't come to you. You will come to me. Don't worry about the rain or the darkness, just come. Meet me in the cemetery, by our stone, and I'll tell you everything we have to do to make our connection powerful. So I can live again.

Nadia wanders towards the door, and she lets herself out, but Erica knows that she'll have no trouble squeezing past the junk that she'd stacked in the hall.

Despite what she tells herself consciously, she knows that she'll do it, and she cannot believe that she's willing to take such a leap. Twenty-four hours sounds too lean to figure out how she'll do what she expects to do without being caught, but she prays that Nadia will help her to figure out the small stuff.

But a deed like this one comes with a truckload of complications, she realizes. The first problem is that she has no idea what she will do with a girl that has returned from the dead. She can take care of Nadia, she can raise her as her own even, but she knows that neither is a viable plan forever. Do resurrected girls grow up the same as other girls? she wonders. She won't find out if she can help it.

Then she worries over what others will say. Small towns breed gossipers the way Nebraska farmers grow corn, she thinks, and decides that a young girl living in her home will kick-start the dirty talk. First the neighbors will whisper to each other until the jabronies a block over know. Soon, everyone in town will want to know the dirt on the girl who has moved into Erica's house out of the blue.

What Michael will say she has considered less, but she knows that she can never convince him that she's doing something completely normal. He's so rigid that way, she thinks, and she hopes that she can sneak this one past him.

Then she considers whether or not she really wants to visit the cemetery. Granted, she finds no other choice in the matter, but she also realizes how few options she's ever had. She also realizes that she has never had a proper relationship with Nadia, and that now is the time to do everything over again. Now that she realizes that she is luckier than most, she wants to have her sister back, no matter what.

*   *   *

Time is running out, Erica thinks, but she knows that she won't be going anywhere as long as she has a greater problem on her hands. When she told Michael her plans, his eyes darted at her, and his face turned red, and she didn't know whether to be scared or amused. He has always been so kind, understanding and loving, and seeing his teeth clenched makes her squirm.

When she creeps into the bedroom, she sees him stuff shirts and pants into a suitcase. The leg of his black dress slacks hang out of the suitcase, but he doesn't bother to tuck it in when he struggles with the suitcase zipper. He mutters random thoughts to himself like Fuck the shaving kit, I'll buy razors and cream at the store. Erica doesn't bother to ask him where he thinks he's going. Best to let him have his tantrum and blow off steam at his brother's, she decides. She knows the inevitable when she sees it.

Just now, she realizes how much Michael reminds her of her father. Dad never stuffed suitcases full of clothes, and he never forgot his shaving kit, but he always blew up any time Erica needed him, or said the first thing that he didn't like. When Erica told Michael that she had a task to complete tonight, he threw a case at the wall. The pieces of shattered porcelain still lay on the wet carpet. Violent yes, and it pains her, but she wasn't startled. Those memories, she thinks. Those very painful memories.

Erica blocks Michael before he can storm out the bedroom door. His shirt is unbuttoned, and his fly hangs at the bottom of his zipper. He looks ready to tear her away from the doorframe if he must, but she won't budge.

Get the hell out of my way. Michael doesn't shout, but his voice sounds low and cracked. She can't remember when he's sounded so cold.

No! she says. Not until you tell me why you're just packing up and walking out the door.

Like you can't figure it out for yourself? he says. Tired of all the head games. Sick and tired of you saying that you're sick and then not bothering to go for treatment so you can get better. Most of all, I'm tired of your stupid flights of fancy.

The last part wasn't what hurt her the most. Really, being told that she had refused treatments wounded her more. That told her that Michael didn't really believe that she was sick and, if that was the case, she will be all alone to fight it.

She has felt stoic up until now, but he has her ready to cry. A lump grows in her throat, and she fights it, but there's no use.

Don't start that now, he says. He jerks left and right like a boxer, to find his way past her, but she won't let him leave her. Not when she's sick.

Why shouldn't I cry? She asks. You just want to leave me now that the going's gotten rough. Guess I know what kind of man you really are Michael.

He bites his bottom lip and says: It's not that and you know it. Don't try and spin this the way you spin everything. Won't work.

And why not?

Because we both know exactly what the problem is here. We both know that you won't take the bull by the friggin' horns and get treatment. If we're going to stay together, and make this work, it's gonna take two of us!

You're just not man enough to stick by me and take on the big problems, are you? she asks.

When he grabs her shoulder, and tears her away from the door, she holds fast to the doorframe, but not enough to stop him from hauling her back. He yanks her back, whips her to the floor, and storms out the door.

She listens as his feet pound the steps and the front door slams. This hurts her, but she forces herself to remain optimistic. On the bright side, she knows that he won't really leave her. Not for good. To her, Michael is behaving like a child who pretends to run away from home, and who will return with his tail tucked between his legs.

While she sits and waits, she loses confidence that he will return, but she chooses not to worry about the minute things now. She has so many greater things to worry about.

For now, all she cares about is doing what Nadia says she must do. And Damn that Michael, she thinks. He's cost me precious time!

Certainly Nadia will forgive her lateness, Erica thinks. After all, she's waited twenty years to strengthen this connection, and return to the living, so she is positive that another hour won't kill her.

*   *   *

Just like Nadia says, Erica arrives at the cemetery, prepared to make their connection powerful again. What the means seems uncertain to her as she figures that it must require more contact than just the touch of their fingertips. The drive over feels tedious, as the radio buzzes static in her ear, but she barely hears it anyway. Noise has become a nuisance so she switches it off.

The church sits next to the graveyard and the stained glass windows are shaded. She checks her watch and realizes that the neighbors should be in bed now, and that no one will see her if she plays it safe. Michael will return home, she knows, but not in time to realize that she's left. When she kills the engine, she switches the headlights off and steps out of the car. Slow, quiet steps into the cemetery must be taken, she realizes, and she hopes she can find the gravestone in the dark. With any luck, Nadia will await her, and lead her back to the car.

Thoughts of full moons, mists and strange noises in the bushes off her mind, she strolls through the cemetery gates, and checks to her left and right, just to be sure that no one will see her.

Without a flashlight, Erica wanders down a gravel path, and searches for her and Nadia's gravestone. She has never been a cemetery person, and she regrets that her last visit to her sister's grave was her burial.

But she forgives me, Erica tells herself. I was a kid, and I'd grown up by the time I could understand what she was going through, what was going to happen to her. After tonight, sorrow won't matter. Only the future is important to her.

A left turn leads her to the river, and she hopes to find the stone before she's late to meet Nadia. Lateness will be less forgivable, she figures.

Towards the older stones, she finds rows of graves with her family's name. She remembers childhood strolls through the cemetery with Mom, and how they always stopped before these one's marked for relatives she'd never met. These trips were never to visit Nadia's grave, but for Mom to remind her of where she's going before long. She never said it in those words, but Mom's silence during those strolls made it clear.

At the stone wall, she finds Nadia, but she doesn't bother to ask why she hasn't waited at her grave. Her color looks much better than it has the last few nights, and she looks like she's spent an hour brushing her hair. Her clothes look like they've come fresh off of the ironing board. For the first time, Nadia cracks a full smile, with cream white teeth, like happiness is on the horizon.

Erica expects to find dirt beneath Nadia's fingernails, like she would try and dig herself out, but she knows how silly that is. Bodies have mattered little to her until now. How Nadia can stand before her now is an answer that she cannot know, she decides. A connection with Nadia's spirit will matter most, she thinks, and she refuses to turn away now.

You made it, just like I knew you would, Nadia says.

Erica inches closer and says: I wouldn't miss this for anything.

You know what must be done.

Erica nods.

First, Nadia says: Take my hand. Make the connection happen, make it real.

Nadia's hand extended, Erica is slow to accept it. She expects Nadia's touch to feel different than it had before, and she doesn't want her reluctance to show. Still, she won't keep Nadia waiting.

When she accepts Nadia's hand, her sister's fingers curl around her hand, but Nadia's hand breaks away, like a gag limb.

She expects to tumble backwards, but she hasn't broken away from Nadia. Her sister stays close by her, with her arm draped over Erica's shoulder. Their feet leave the grass and the float above the cemetery like they are filled with helium.

What's happening? Erica gasps and clutches to Nadia. Where are you taking me?

You made the connection, Nadia says, and I'll take care of the rest. We'll be taking a little detour I didn't tell you about. Sorry if I led you on, but life will be much better this way. Count on it.

But I'm still human and I can't hang on to you forever! Won't I fall?

Nadia smiles and says: Don't you realize that nothing bad can happen to you up here? This is how I've lived since I lost my life and I want you to live with me in a world without pain and sorrow.

Erica feels confused. If her job is to save Nadia, that plan is all but abandoned. She realizes that if Nadia has saved her that she must now follow her lead.

Remember your back pain? Nadia asks, like she knows that her slip on an icy sidewalk at seventeen has kept her in physiotherapy ever since. Tell me, she says, your back bother you now?

Only then does Erica realize that her aches and pains have vanished. She's felt nothing aside from fear and confusion since they ascended from the earth and she wonders why her sister would trick her like this. Childish games, she figures.

Erica says: I don't feel the pain anymore, but you should've told me the truth from the start. We have to trust each other to share a life together, right?

Nadia winks then says: Don't be so dramatic, 'sis. It's for your own good.

Erica realizes how adult-like Nadia sounds and she feels her own authority slip away. I never had any control over the situation anyway, she tells herself.

Okay, Erica says, can you tell me *why* you tried to trick me?

You've never be free of your life by yourself. You need to live in a place where you can be happy, but we both know that would never happen unless you've got me around. You know, in your daily life? It took some doing, let me tell you, but man have I got those wheels turning!

Just then, she realizes that she won't return to her old life. Michael is gone, and when he returns as she believes he will, he will find an empty bed and driveway. Worry he will, she realizes, but she decides that it's immaterial. Nothing can hurt her now.

Tell me more about this new life, Erica says.

That cancer of yours, Nadia says. Consider it gone. No treatments, no radiation, no surgery and, best of all, no catch. Here's your clean bill of health, 'sis.

But that can't . . . . Erica doesn't bother to finish as she knows that Nadia will reassure her that it everything can be true. To her, anything is possible now.

Like her twin is a fairy godmother, Erica wants to pull her in closer, but she doesn't dare disrupt her when they're this high up.

She wants to fight back tears, but she also knows that tears won't exist where they're going.

Where they're going . . . . Erica doesn't know where that is, but knowing that she'll be there with Nadia is all that matters. She could be headed for heaven, or some nameless place. Names are meaningless to her.

As they peer upon what they leave behind, Erica has no regrets. No longer is she angry at Nadia for deceiving her, and now is glad. She realizes that their connection is no mistake and that she will not take it back for anything.

Heaven seems like such a mild word as they enter the light. Erica has never believed that such a place exists, at least not as others say it does. Still, it is a peaceful place, and that she is here with Nadia makes it perfect.

*   *   *

Michael sits across from a man in a suit, who wears glasses, a brown moustache, and a smile. The desk between them is small enough for Richards to take Michael's hand if he wants to. Men like him can always set him at ease, Michael thinks, but he knows that he must live with a host of unanswered questions anyway.

Take your time, Richards says. I don't want to rush you when you've got this much on your plate.

Never one to confide in another, including Erica, Michael decides that Richards will need to sit tight for now. He shifts a little and Richards' eyes follow him. Michael says: Bet you've seen a lot in your business. Does this ever make people paranoid? I mean, do they ever worry that they're burying their spouse alive?

Richards inches closer, like he wants to take Michael's hand then backs off. He says: To be honest, that's the first time I've heard someone say that, and there's not much left for anyone to say that can surprise me. But I can't say that they don't experience those feelings deep down. I can't read their minds, after all.

Michael combs his fingers through his hair and says: I know. It's just that damn autopsy report. If it's just given me some answers, and I didn't have to live with all this inconclusive crap, I could just bury Erica and get this over with.

Richards nods, like he understands, but Michael knows that his years in the funeral business cannot prepare him to tell a story like this. Society's separation from emotion hasn't caused his dilemma as much as his own distance from his emotions has. If I seem like a cold fish, so be it, he decides.

Michael remembers the night he walked out on her, and how he checked into a motel, but barely had time to switch the television on before heading back home. He is sure that he could've saved her had he never left, but he wonders if anything could have really saved her. She might've slipped away had he slept next to her and he would have been none the wiser.

When he left, he remembers that Erica seemed so convinced that he would return, that he wouldn't really leave her, that the act became near impossible. Years of insisting that she was sick had driven him out the door, so far as he was concerned, and yet he didn't want to abandon the girl he loved. At the very least, he reminds himself, he tried to find her the help that she needed, even if Erica sought help for every illness save for the one in her mind. Michael wishes now that he had been more direct, forceful even, or that he had staged an intervention.

Back in the car, he knows that coming home means that he must concede to Erica, but he decides that it will be worth it. He's put him with plenty up to this point, he thinks, and he wants to see her through the rest.

When he flips the light on, he thinks that Erica has fallen asleep, but when he speaks her name, she doesn't move. A gentle nudge doesn't wake her. He checks her pulse, feels nothing, and then freezes.

For a moment, he wishes that he would've listened to her when she complained of her health problems, but later he tells himself that no one could've taken her seriously. People die suddenly, he realizes, despite their age, and he sucks it up and sees to the practical matters. He calls 911, an ambulance arrives, and the neighbors stand on their lawns in pajamas, robes, and curlers, to watch the commotion. Several productions have come from Michael's house in the last few years and he is surprised to see that the neighbors' fascination hasn't died.

When the medics instruct Michael to follow them to the hospital, he nods and grabs his coat, but he checks the room for anything that might've killed her. He finds no bottle of pills and no alcohol, and he hopes that depression hasn't caught up with her.

At the hospital, a doctor tells Michael just what the medics have told him, which is what he has known from the start. Michael assures the doctor that he had walked in and found Erica in bed, and that he has found nothing to suggest that she has committed suicide. The doctor says that an autopsy will be performed, and that it should provide him answers, and peace of mind.

Michael daydreams, as a doctor cuts Erica open, and he worries that she might wake, and find a red, dripping Y on her chest. That's not so silly, he thinks. Inconclusive results return, and Michael is not surprised. After the last few years, and the hell that he has gone through with Erica, he decides that it's the only appropriate way for them to part. But he wonders if anything Erica said was true. Just for a moment.

The doctor rests his hand on Michael's shoulder, like that helps, and says that he's sorry. Big fucking help you are, Michael thinks. The doctor tells him that space is tight and that he must call a funeral home. Just then, Michael realizes that he can't call. Only then does it dawn on him that he will need to, but he knows that his wife isn't dead. No doubt they'll say that he is in denial, or that Erica's death hasn't sunk in with him yet, but he knows that it's crap. Had they lived the last few years with Erica, they would leave science behind, he is certain.

Now in Richards' office, he worries that he will spill everything. He wonders if he should wait to sell the book and film rights, but emotions matter more to him than anything. He feels more detached from his feelings than ever, but he never expected them to matter.

Richards finally pats Michael's hand, and Michael doesn't pull back. Richards says: Just because I haven't seen your case before doesn't mean that there aren't others who can relate. I've donated books on grieving and loss to the public library. Not sure what they bought with the money I gave them, but I bet they'll have something that you can identify with.

Oh, they won't, Michael thinks, but he doesn't want to challenge Richards when he's trying to help him.

Michael says: All this time she spent thinking she was sick, that she had cancer, and I didn't think anything would really happen to her. And when something finally *does* come along, and takes her away from me, I can't even know what that something is.

Richards nods.

Her parents, Michael says. Her Mom and Dad treated her like shit and she was in a funk about it as long as I've known her, but who holds onto this stuff for so long?

If I have a single regret, Michael says, it's that I didn't play along with the little things the way I could have. Like all this business about a twin sister. I didn't have patience for a grown woman with an imaginary friend, okay? Not with the careers that we both wanted, and the lifestyles that would've come with it. But there's a point when you do what you've got to do. So if I'd just gone along with it . . would it have killed me?

Richards doesn't nod this time, but Michael knows that he must understand. If he has a wife, he must know that he can't be the perfect husband. Still, Richards couldn't have experienced this. Not in a life in which he is married to two women, and in which the balance of power has always leaned in favor of the woman he cannot see. This woman is all powerful, has the key to life and death, and the strength to make a connection from the beyond.

Home Again

I'm not a bad guy. Really I'm not. But I've done some bad shit in my time, I can tell you that. Well, just one bad thing actually. I don't feel bad about it either. The only way to rationalize my absence of guilt is to offer an explanation. So don't judge me yet. Hear me out.

You know me. That is, if you watch daytime television. You have seen my mug plastered all over the tube, the net and even a few tabloids. Nothing major. Still, I've had a taste of what fame can bring. I never thought anyone would give a damn about who I was dating, if I'm single or if I'm circumcised, but life can surprise you. Sorry but I won't tell you my name or the name of the soap opera I appeared in. I'm here to rationalize my deeds, not to get myself thrown in the big house. For the purposes of this story, just call me Mike.

I grew up in a small town and I'm not afraid to say that I like that town. So it was a natural place for me to return after I lost my job on the show. No, I didn't do anything wrong. I didn't tell off the boss or perform any of the defiant acts that people in menial 9-5 jobs would kill to do. My character was one that never ages. You know what I'm talking about? The producers simply hire a younger—and sometimes better-looking—actor to play the part every five years or so. I had been hired to that part after my predecessor in the role had ages and I guess I was naive enough to believe that it wouldn't happen to me. But that's not the important stuff. That's the icing on the cake to make myself sound more interesting. No doubt you're already racking your brain to try and figure out who I am.

What's important to this story is what I did after my time with the show ended. That's why you're reading this, right? Without any further adieu . . . .

I'm a murderer, plain and true. No, not a murderer of the O.J. variety. His victims didn't deserve it. My victim—Steve, we'll him—deserved it all right. Even though I can trace most of my animosity back to one major incident, it wasn't about any one act that he had committed. It was all of the feelings that festered thanks to his behaviour. All of the resentment boiled.

So Steve and I grew up together. We went to the same pre-school together, the same grade school and ultimately the same high school. We were both the odd kid out, you could say. I had my looks, which were marginal then and developed as I matured and landed me my soap opera gig, but neither of us was a beacon of popularity. We had each other and you could argue that we needed each other all the same.

They say that you can't defend the things that you did in high school, and I guess that goes double for the things that you did in elementary school. Steve had always been an asshole. He was your friend one minute and Satan himself the next. That was just in his makeup and he would have you know it too, even if it was just to excuse his ridiculous behaviour. Sometimes he would oversleep through a planned get together and other times he would simply no-show without a phone call.

But the ridicule . . . that's what grinded my gears more than anything. I said that Steve was your best friend one minute and Satan himself the next, that's true, but his devilish side appeared most often when we were in the company of others. And if Steve wanted to impress those people—look out!

Indeed, when others were around, he would stick his hand out to them and say, "Hi, my name is Mike, and by the way, I'm going to acting school!"

And then the laugh would come. It was a loud, high-pitched hyena-like laugh that would have been comical if it hadn't been so goddamned obnoxious.

Of course, that wasn't the only barb. It was only one in a series of insults. Others came when I was talking to the same people he'd wanted to impress. Sometimes they would ask me how my parents were doing, or how acting school was treating me, so I would tell them. Steve's laughter availed itself, loud and shrill, so much that I and the person engaging me would wonder what the hell was wrong with him.

"Hey Mike," Steve would say. "Why don't you shut the fuck up? Nobody cares about your little acting school!"

The sentence, of course, was accompanied by another chorus of laughter.

And obviously the person I was talking to cared about how acting school was going for me. They wouldn't have asked if they hadn't, right?

I know what you're thinking: if they guy was such an asshole, why remain friends with him? And you have a very valid point. My personal philosophy was very much intact before I became successful, which is to treat others the way I would like to be treated. The golden rule. Very simple, right? I'd decided that a friend is someone that knows all of your faults and likes you anyway. I mean, it's not like the guy was without some endearing qualities. And it's not like I'm perfect either.

As time passed, I realized that the guy was like a drug. I knew that he was bad for me, and I knew that should have pushed him away, and yet I just couldn't bring myself to do it. And, funny enough, Steve was the one to pull the plug on me. I thought that maybe I should have considered his severing of our relationship to have been a blessing in disguise. That wasn't hindsight either. I'd thought it from the start. There's much more to it than that, which I will explain shortly, dear reader.

I bet you think that our falling out was the result of a disagreement or some astronomical blowout. Nope. In fact, our parting of the ways was rooted in nothing at all. We had exchanged some e-mails—the son of a bitch never answered the phone to anyone during the best of times—and he'd told me how much he wanted to get together with me.

On most planets, such an e-mail would have been an invitation to follow up. But not on Steve's. After a month of silence, I sent him a series of follow up e-mails until he finally sent an angry return message. I won't bore you with the details. It was as confusing as all get out.

Had I done something wrong? I hadn't thought so. Even Steve's e-mail, angry though it was, didn't point to any wrongdoing on my part. I should have taken that chapter's end as liberating. Really, it was my permission to move on from someone who'd dragged me to the bottom of a sea of negativity. But not everything makes sense. Not everything is cut, dry and neat.

Then the dreams started. Not nightmares, but they were horrible in their own right. Sometimes I dreamed about the old days, when everything had been as fine as paint between us. In some dreams, we were teenagers, and in others we were in our early twenties, getting into wilder, more drunken mischief. And sometimes I had dreamed about him grinding his barbs into my flesh, nice and deep. Though Steve had been slipping his shots in—and it'd pissed me off royally—I still suffered from a tremendous sense of loss.

Obviously the wounds ran deeper than I was willing to admit. I felt betrayed. Others in the same position will relate even if they're unwilling to admit it. But the chapter was closed, or so I'd thought. But he did and I'd wanted him to more than I could have realized.

*   *   *

So I got fired. No, that's too harsh of a term. My contract wasn't renewed and I knew precisely why. They wanted a younger actor to keep that character looking youthful and sexy. That's show biz for you. It chews you up and spits you out. My agent assured me that he would find me new work in a flash, but I didn't want to work. Not right away. Maybe that sounds crazy, but filming a daily soap opera is demanding and I just wanted to rest.

My former co-workers on the show thought I was crazy for returning to the town where I'd grown up. The show was filmed in New York and they must have expected that I would be unable to shake the faux sophistication that living in a midtown Manhattan apartment had instilled in me. But the truth is that I missed the quiet living and the familiar faces of people that always have time for small talk.

I rented an apartment in town; just something temporary. If I wanted to move on sooner than I had anticipated, I could just sublet the place. The apartment that I chose was the nicest that I could find. Since the town wasn't brimming with apartment buildings, my choices were limited. The building was populated mostly by seniors, which suited me just fine. Call me crazy, but I didn't want to wind up in some dump with the dregs of society.

The dreams that I'd had worsened when I'd returned to town, and that shouldn't have come as a surprise. I was back in the same town with Steve who I hadn't seen or heard from since I'd been in acting school. He could have been dead for all I'd known or cared. But I hadn't been that lucky, that was for sure.

I doubted that I would have needed to worry about bumping into him either. The last I knew of him, the guy slept for 12 hours a day, and seldom left his house. If he had a job, I would have been stunned. Steve was the vice president of lazy and tigers never change their stripes.

As it'd turned out, I had been wrong on the most important of those points. I *did* run into Steve. Well, I didn't run into him exactly. It wasn't a chance meeting. How he knew I was back in town much less where I was living was a mystery to me, but news travels fast in small communities.

When my buzzer sounded, and his voice turned up on the other end, I thought that someone was playing a prank on me. But it was Steve all right. His voice and tenor hadn't changed nor should it have after just a few years. A wave of confusion washed over me. Why was he here? Did he think I'd forgotten the way he'd treated me? So I buzzed him up to my apartment. Maybe you would have told someone like him to go the hell, but I just didn't have the nerve. And besides, I'd thought that it was an opportunity to clear up some unanswered questions.

I'd needed time to prep myself for this, so I didn't wait at the door for him. What would I say to him? I'd wondered. Deep down, I'd wanted to tell him where to get off the moment he darkened my door, but there was no sense in that. We weren't in high school anymore for God's sake. There had been no reason to be childish. Most importantly, I couldn't have let him see how deeply he'd wounded me.

Then he tapped on my door. My hand quaked as I gripped the knob. Why should I have been so nervous? And why should I have given a shit about this guy? Frankly, I don't know. The human mind and heart are quirky little things and you can never make sense of them.

When I opened the door, I found a plumper Steve than the one I had remembered. Seven years changes everyone, I guess. And maybe it shouldn't have come as a surprise even though the kid had been hopelessly scrawny the last time I'd seen him. Steve was a layabout and he scarfed down fast food on a daily basis. That shit catches up with you, I don't care who you are.

"H-h-hey!" Steve shouted. "Long time no see!"

He stuck his hand out; I accepted it reluctantly. And then he hugged me as if no years had passed, as if he had never left me high and dry, and as if no vile e-mail had ever entered cyberspace.

"Come on in and make yourself comfortable," I said.

Steve wandered through the apartment like he'd never seen such a grand place in his entire life. That, of course, was bullshit. It was a regular two bedroom apartment. But maybe it was a palace to a man who was practically a hermit in his own home.

"I heard you were back in town," Steve said. "So I wanted to make sure I stopped by to pay you a visit."

"How did you know where I live?"

"Your folks told me. Man, haven't talked to them in ages either. They're looking great and so are you!"

That was the most insincere pile of crap I'd ever heard. I'd never forgotten about how he'd once loved to disparage my parents to my face. So why had he come to see me? I'd wondered. Maybe he'd thought I was rich. I'm not rich but I'm comfortable by anyone's standards. Steve had always been one to know which bandwagon to latch onto. He had once told me that he always considered the pros and cons in that regard. And now that I had become moderately successful, he had placed me in the 'pro' category, and had latched himself onto my bandwagon, thus ending his seven years of silence.

"So, you must have a ton to talk about," Steve said.

"Oh yeah, lots. But I get tired of talking about myself. Let's talk about you and how you've been doing. Last I knew you wanted to go back to school and become a baker's apprentice or something."

Steve waved his hand. "Gave that up. Just wasn't for me."

"Just one semester, eh?"

"No, no, just one week. God, those early classes were ball busters."

The more things changed, the more they stayed the same, I thought.

*   *   *

"You know how big of a bitch it is to get up at eight a.m. for a ten a.m. class? Unbelievable."

I wanted to regale him about how hard it is to spend twelve hours a day on a soap opera set only to crash on the sofa in your dressing room, but I didn't want to be confrontational. That's never been my strong suit.

"So you're still living in town, I take it?" I asked.

"Oh yeah, still living in the same house, trying like crazy to get out of it. I'm gonna be moving to the big city soon. I was supposed to move to Mexico last year, but I ran into a big cluster-fuck with this girl and it really screwed me up bad."

I could barely resist the urge to shake my head in disgust. Steve was the same old leech that he'd always been, but silly me for thinking that he'd changed.

"This place is awesome!" Steve smiled. "I bet you've been banging a million gals in this place!"

Right then I thought that I'd been warped back to high school. Indeed, I'd bedded my share of beautiful women in New York, and had kept select company since returning home, but I saw no reason to brag. Numbers weren't everything to me. Women weren't everything to me either.

After the interlude at my apartment, Steve enticed me to join him for dinner. We visited Romeo's, one of our old haunts, and a stellar place for all things Italian. That he would expect me to pick up the bill had occurred to me. The waitress could be assured of a tip that way, I decided. After a meal of pizza and wings, Steve did leave me with the bill. I shrugged it off the way I had shrugged off all of his ignorance since he had walked back into my life.

But through it all, I was happy to see him. I might have had to contend with his ridiculous humor and his fantasies about moving to the big city, but the hold that Steve had ripped in my heart had been mended. And yet life was far from perfect. I wanted my friend back, but I didn't want to be turned into the unrefined image of our younger selves. I could never resume my career, and could never succeed again as long as Steve was tied to my leg like a boulder. I just didn't know which path to choose.

*　*　*

After our dinner at Romeo's, Steve phone and texted me daily, but I saw him in the flesh more often than not. We ate out, went to the movies, and even took a road trip to Cleveland. All of those activities had been on my dime, of course. Rick, my agent, called me to say that he had lined up some new opportunities for me. After six months out of the game, I needed work. And I was rested. But I didn't feel motivated to audition for those roles.

Rick, who had represented me since I'd broken into the business, told me in no uncertain terms to shape my ass up. I had been dealt a shitty break in the soap opera business, he'd continued, and other directors and producers could forgive that, but I couldn't just blow off golden opportunities while they were staring me right in the face.

He said that he was hanging up now and that he would give me some time to think about it. I promised him I would. But I mostly sat around on my ass, feeling miserable, quite frankly. And, on top of that, the dreams had started up again. These dreams about Steve were different from the old ones. In these dreams, I had become just like him. I had no job, no ambition and nothing to look forward to. All I could do was leech off of successful people.

Hell, I figured Steve would abandon me again once he found one that what little fame I'd garnered was dissipating, and that my once comfortable bank account was nearly drained. That would have been appropriate, wouldn't it? But then I would have been plagued by dreams of Steve leaving me again. I couldn't win.

On the other hand, I couldn't let my career go to dross. I'd worked too long and too hard to get where I am to let an absolute loser ruin it for me. Then the crime entered my mind. It sounded great, but could I really do it? I didn't think so. I was scared to death and yet I swore I had no other choice.

And no, it wasn't something that I did right away. Haste makes waste, as they say. There's no way I could have pulled it off much less gotten away with it if I'd rushed it. I'm still skeptical about writing this confession.

We took a drive along the river one night. That had been a relaxing pastime of ours when we were in our late teens. If we weren't out drinking and partying on a Friday night, we played it low-key by driving and cranking up the music.

As it'd turned out, he wasn't going to move to the big city after all. Plans had changed. What a big fucking surprise that was. That had triggered the drive. He had called me because the girl whom he'd met for a few coffee dates didn't want to see him anymore, leaving him in rough shape.

Before, I would have been a dummy; I would have let him pour his heart out to me and I might have even sympathized with him. But not this time. I wouldn't let him make a dummy out of me again and I meant to take matters into my own hands.

It was summer and, instead of cranking up the air conditioning, we rolled down the windows and let the wind rip through the car. Steve had compiled a new CD of tunes that I really liked and slid it into the player. That really sucked given what I had planned to do to him.

I pulled into a parking lot along the river then shut off the headlights and killed the engine. Night had fallen and we had driven out far enough that no one would see us. There was no trail where we walked, just grass, mud and a shit load of rocks.

I'd never owned a knife (or a gun for that matter) until I'd planned the murder. Once the seed had been planted, I bought a knife, and tucked it neatly in a sheath beneath my clothes. My legs quaked and I felt sick. I wanted to do it, but I didn't know if I could. What's more, I didn't know if I could get away with it. If I was sloppy, the police would catch me instantly and I would spend the rest of my life behind bars. How's that for revenge?

"So I need to know," Steve said. "Do you think I should make a Plan B or see if I can make some magic work with this girl?"

"I don't fucking know." I combed my fingers through my hair. "I've been trying to tell you that women are bad news. The ones to chase go for are, at least. If you really want to be happy, you're just going to have to think about the kind of girls you've been chasing and ask yourself if it's worth the bullshit."

Steve's brow furrowed. He had noticed the frustration in my voice, as had I. Frankly, I couldn't take any more of his problems. And that isn't to say that I wasn't willing to be there for a friend in need, but Steve refused to acknowledge the answers that had stared him right in the face. It was infuriating.

"You got a problem, man?" Steve asked. His tone was reminiscent of the old days when he'd had a bone to pick with me. His classic line had been *Back off, man!!*the second I'd offended him with the truth.

"No, no problem," I said, "but you've got to look yourself in the mirror, right? The only person that can take control of your life is you and I think it's time you did it."

"Hey, fuck you, pal! You think it's easy to get women when you're regular old me?" Then he reverted to his mimicking mode while dancing around like an idiot. "Oh, fiddle-dee-dee! Would you look at me? I'm Mike, the soap opera star that couldn't cut it. I'm such a fucking big shot!"

The more that behavior continued, the more intensely I longed to unleash the knife and do my worst. I stared deep into his eyes. God how I hated Steve's ridiculous expression. I loathed it and I always had. It was time to free myself from Steve once and for all.

I wound up and slugged Steve in the face so quickly that he hadn't known it was coming. He dropped to the mud like a sack of potatoes, but he did not lay flat. No, he rolled around in the muck like his clothes were on fire then clung onto my pant legs and dragged me down with him. Yes, I should have been more attentive, and I should have moved in on him the second he was down, but I'd never struck anyone before much less murdered them.

I'd stayed in good shape owing to upcoming auditions. Steve, on the other hand, had fallen into serious disrepair. Only the raw strength that'd come with his weight gain was to his advantage. He tried to topple me, but I managed to roll him over and pin him down.

His eyes bulged out, and his fingernails dug into my flesh, until I unsheathed my knife.

Then he went impotent, like he meant to surrender right then and there. Tears wept from his eyes and he whimpered.

"P-p-please don't," he said. "Are you fucking crazy?"

Of course I wasn't crazy. I had never seen more clearly in my entire life. Mercy is for the weak, I'd decided. If I would ever be successful again, I must be strong.

So I dug the tip of the knife into his neck's far side, near the jaw. Even sharp knives didn't make quick work of a victim, so I ground the knife into his flesh. I sliced his skin until I had created a wide red, weeping smile from ear to ear. Steve gargled and tried to scream, but his slashed throat wouldn't allow it. He swiped at me a bunch of times too, and even managed to knock the knife from my hand, but it was pointless. I guess it's nature to try and survive despite the odds.

Have you ever seen someone die? It isn't nearly as dramatic as you would expect. Steve struggled at first, but then he slowed to a halt and finally went still. And that was it. The difference between life and death was defined by silence and stillness.

I checked his pulse to make sure he was actually dead and not unconscious. And he was dead all right, not that unconsciousness would have mattered where he was going. I stripped his clothes off, dragged him into the river and set him afloat. Surely he would resurface before the police or some fisherman upriver.

I washed up in the river. Correction, I knelt down to vomit and *then* I washed up in the river. That was my first, last and only murder and the surge of adrenaline had overwhelmed me. You would be amazed at how much of a bitch it is to wash blood off of your hands. The act feels endless. After, I threw Steve's clothes and the knife into the garbage bag I'd brought. I sealed it with a second bag to avoid leaking blood everywhere. Then I added my t-shirt, jeans and shoes and drove home in my underwear to avoid tracking blood into the car.

Steve turned up on the news two days later. His body had drifted to a marina a few miles south of where I'd killed him. I pictured his pale, bloated corpse as the cops fished him out of the water. The news station said that the police were investigating a homicide but had no leads. Whenever anyone asked, I pretended to be as shocked as they were. I even cried at the funeral.

Like I told you, I'm not a bad guy. I'm really not. But I did what I needed to do. The dreams ceased instantly and presumably forever.

And now I'm in Hollywood, having performed in several romantic comedies. I might never win an Oscar, but that's life. Steve's murder was business that I'd had to see to, otherwise I would have been nothing, and Steve would have dragged me to that state. And now that Steve is gone, and I have written my confession, I can close the book on him forever.

Derek Clendening lives in Fort Erie, Ontario. In addition to this work, he has also written *The Between Years* and *The Vampire Way* available from Naked Snake Press.